The Long Journey Home

The Long Journey Home

A Collection of Short Stories

Lawrence Dorr

Högalid Press
Reno, Nevada

Högalid Press
4790 Caughlin Pkwy St. 317
Reno, Nevada 89519
www.hogalidpress.com

ISBN – 13: 978-0982987223
ISBN – 10: 0982987226
Library of Congress Control Number: 2013933078

Printed in the United States of America

Dedicated to my beloved children: Sibet and Jim, and
John and Anne

Contents

Pushkin 1

Tossed by the Elephants 15

Stress Test 25

Risen Indeed 33

Verity Unseen 43

A Fable 53

Kate, Kate 59

All Loves Excelling 75

Libera me, Domine, de morte aeterna 87

The Storage Shed 101

A Book of Amos 117

Before the Mountains Were Born 123

Transformations 139

An Eagle's Cry 157

Glory of All Lands 163

A Curse on Details 189

The Sound of Many Waters 199

The Long Journey Home 207

PUSHKIN

The wind swirling trash on Kirov Street, the main thoroughfare of the district of Perchersk—an extension of Kiev—rose unhindered from the Dnieper, the river masking the smell of war, a mixture of the exhaust fumes of trucks, tanks, mobile artillery pieces, horses, wet uniforms, field kitchens, dead bodies rotting under collapsed masonry, and the smell that shook him with fear: the odor of singed hair and burned bodies. Earlier, when he reported in at the field hospital to receive his second typhus shot—they were given at three-day intervals—the ambulances were bringing in burned tank crews.

He was looking in his guidebook for the location of the Pushkin statue. The guidebook, supplied by the Wermacht, was a testimony to German respect for things cultural. What other invading army would have provided its soldiers with tourist information? It was also the pentimento that was supposed to render their barbarism opaque. Serving alongside the German

Army with the 39th Hungarian Tank Regiment had made it easy for him to get hold of the guidebook. He was fluent in German, partly because his boyhood discipline—up to the age of thirteen—had been meted out by a beloved nanny, a Bavarian spinster, and partly because it was one of the required languages, besides Latin and Italian, in his gymnasium. He spoke Russian too, which he had learned at his mother's insistence from a refugee who had been a lady-in-waiting in the last Tsar's court. Madame Ivanovna was hired as his Russian tutor and his mother's 'companion'. His mother and Madame Ivanovna spoke French and practiced English together. Other than his father, nobody at their settlement understood English. Madame Ivanovna was given a small house built of adobe brick like those of the sharecroppers, where she recreated Russia with her icons, samovar, candles, strange smells, a portrait of her dead husband in his general's uniform, and vodka that she drank from a water glass. She played the balalaika, and when she was inebriated cried and called him "my son". He had become a substitute for the child Madame Ivanovna never had. She had told him tales about her life at the Romanov Court, her wedding to the general witnessed by the tsar and the tsarina, moonlight sled rides, balls where she had danced with Tsar Nicholas. Though she was born at least two generations after Pushkin, she spoke about his many duels as if she had been his contemporary, explaining that though the poet died defending the honor of his wife, most of his duels were fought over trivia because he was touchy about his short stature and dark complexion, even if he was proud of his African heritage. Pushkin's maternal grandfather was a slave from Abyssinia who was adopted by Peter the Great and ended up a general in the Russian Army. The stories of the duels made him feel close to Pushkin.

2

His own father also fought duels, one of which was with a music critic who had compared a family friend, the aging American coloratura Galli-Curci, to "a great, very great violinist playing on a wreck of a fiddle with constantly sagging strings." His father had cut off the music critic's left ear and as a consequence had to spend two weeks in the Marko Street jail. Civil law forbade dueling.

It was in Madame Ivanovna's house where he was introduced to Pushkin's poetry. Her reading of the narrative poems with their sad tales made them both cry. He identified especially with Aleko, the betrayed hero in *The Gypsies* who kills his beloved and her lover.

"She is a child,/(the Old Man said.) *And you should treat her moods more lightly./To you, love is a serious business,/But a girl's heart treats it as a joke./ Look up: look at the distant moon;/She sheds an equal radiance/On everything she passes over."*

Six months before a caravan had halted next to the settlement to trade work—mending pots and pans—for a few older horses. There was a gypsy girl among them who had become his friend. His mother had called the girl 'my son's impossible love'. Then one day he saw the girl lift her skirts to a gypsy man.

At eighteen he entered the national military academy, where in a year-and-a-half instead of the usual four years, his class earned the gold star of lieutenancy and was sent to the Eastern Front.

* * * * * *

He had reached Kirov Street from the Dneprovsky Descent, walking around German military trucks, some filled with artillery shells, some with gasoline containers. There were also white ambulances with red crosses painted on them pulled halfway up on the sidewalks. A company of panzer grenadiers marched past him on their way toward their temporary barracks in the Mariinsky Palace. He had heard rumors of a beginning Russian counter-offensive around Kursk and Belgorod about 400 kilometers east of Kiev, but there were still too many German soldiers out on passes for the rumors to be true. This was the first time he had been to Russia but his ancestors had been here. On his mother's side a junior officer in Napoleon's Grand Army had survived the 1812 retreat to settle later in Alsace-Lorraine. He knew from history books that his Cuman ancestors on his father's side had sacked Kyiv, as it was called in 1202 AD, before they themselves were chased all the way to Hungary in 1242 by Batu Khan's Golden Horde. The stories he had heard about Kuthan, the valiant Cuman Chief who led their tribe to Hungary, were told by his grandfather sitting on feed sacks in the barn. When he had asked his father if the stories were true, his father had said that they were legends handed down through many generations, and that they probably had a historical basis. It was then that his father showed him the dark, oiled dog-skin parchment of their land grant from 1305.

* * * * * *

Three months ago in July his regiment had entrained at the Kolomyva railhead—tanks on flat beds, the crews in nicely fixed-up boxcars with bunk-beds and even a woodstove for cooking and heat. For the first time in his life he was traveling without a nanny or a tutor. He liked to slide the loading door halfway back to look at the countryside and at the little stations slowly moving backward while the languorous clicking of the wheels counted down the passing *versts* transforming him into a Tolstoy character journeying in a *troika*. He was here in the land of Chekhov, Dostoevski, Turgenev and most of all, Pushkin, whose poetry had

4

consumed him even at the military academy where he was taught in his truncated courses only the use of weapons and tactics. The train traveling on its wide tracks moved slowly enough for the mosquitoes to land on his forehead but it also enabled him to see the people, mostly women, as they halted momentarily at their work to straighten up and look back at him, their faces framed by babushkas of many colors. In the distance farm carts created a continuous dust curtain as a backdrop to set the stage for Pushkin. *"Summer, your beauty, I would be in love/ With you, if it were not for the heat, dust, flies,/Mosquitoes."*

Then it happened as any sane person living in the reality of the Eastern Front of 1943 knew it would happen. While the train was slowing down passing Vinnytsa, a small pineapple landed at his feet with a dull thud. He knew pineapples only from pictures, never having held one in his hands. The same applied to enemy hand grenades. When his brain finally gave the command, his right leg moved like a slow-motion knee articulation study, then the toe of his boot connected and the grenade flew out in an arc, slowly losing height before exploding above the ground.

* * * * * *

The park, crisscrossed by trenches dug at the order of the Red Army before they retreated from Kiev, made it difficult to pretend that he was here only to search for Madame Ivanovna's beloved friend. Then not far from the park he saw a marble column supporting a seated Aleksandr Sergeevich Pushkin. The gold paint of the Cyrillic letters carved into the marble shone in the late September sunshine. At nineteen degrees Celsius there was no hint of the horrors of the Russian winter that was to come. He looked up at the seated figure, willing it to speak, remembering his French grandfather's story about Michelangelo bringing down his hammer on the head of his just-finished statue of Moses, shouting: "Speak!" The granite figure didn't resemble Madame Ivanovna's little oval painting of Pushkin even though the curly hair and beard that left his chin naked emphasizing his full lips, were chiseled into the stone. In the painting his blue eyes looked at the world with bafflement, a sad stare that as a boy he thought he understood. The carving with its sightless eyes was a death mask. He didn't know if it was hysteria or premonition that made him feel that he stood on a verge, the rim of a chasm, waiting for the push that would make him dive into oblivion. He looked up at Pushkin, only a head and shoulders above him and heard the familiar voice of Madame Ivanovna reciting: "*I say goodbye to each day,/Trying to guess/Which among them will be/The anniversary of my death. And how and where shall I die?/Fighting, traveling, in the waves?/Or will the neighboring valley/Receive my cold dust?*"

It was then that he saw the girl. She came from behind the column to where he stood. She was below his eye level; the top of her head would barely reach his chin. Incongruously, his first thought was that if he were standing in the turret of his Panzer Kampfwagen IV she could sneak in below the level at which the tank's machine guns could be depressed to fire.

"It doesn't look like Pushkin," he said.

"You speak Russian!" She had long blond hair tied back with a pale yellow scarf.

"So do you."

She burst out laughing. "But I *am* Russian. I'm not German."

"I am not either."

"But you are wearing a German uniform."

"It's not German. I am a lieutenant in the Hungarian Army."

"It is good that you are interested in our Eternal Poet."

"Only God is eternal. Pushkin is dead. Chances are I'll soon be dead too."

That was the beginning. He told her all about Madame Ivanovna and their reading together *The Gypsies, The Bronze Horseman, Mozart and Salieri, Rusalka* and the shorter poems. They were walking side by side on Kirov Street away from Pushkin, passing a church then turning onto another street back toward the park. From time to time the girl's face was turned up toward him like a sunflower. Reaching out for her hand made him conscious of the soldiers, civilians, men, women and even children who walked around them as if the two had become a single obstacle in their path. From the comments he overheard from the Germans and from the looks directed toward them by the civilians, their walking together was judged offensive. He still remembered his mother's remark about the gypsy girl, that it was childish for him to think that a fourteen- year-old gypsy girl could become the friend of a twelve-year-old Hungarian boy. Perhaps it was equally childish for him to think that he loved this girl he had met only a half-an-hour ago. But Romeo and Juliet had only seen each other across a dance floor and had fallen in love in spite their feuding families. Life expectancy for tank crews was three weeks. He would soon be covered in darkness the way the City was plunged into total darkness two days ago when the power plant was blown up by the partisans.

They had stopped. "Can you tell me your name?"

"Lybed Osipnova Lihoded."

"It's a lovely name."

"Lybed was the name of the girl who founded Kiev with her three brothers."

* * * * * *

7

There was only one bench left in the park. Its back had been sawed off to turn it into a weapons' platform. Straddling it they sat down facing each other. He was peering at her face as if looking at a distant star through a telescope. Her nose looked as if at the time of its fashioning the clay had been pinched just the slightest bit to keep it out of true alignment. Her nostrils didn't quite match either. For some unfathomable reason this made him love her even more.

A Hungarian cavalry sergeant passing by gave him an elaborate salute and an unmilitary wink. They knew each other. The sergeant was in the 1st Cavalry Squadron of the 2nd Army that was part of the III Corps as was his own 30th Tank Regiment. He often went to visit the 1st Cavalry's remounts, having ridden them at home at the settlement before they were sold to the Army.

"Are you allowed to tell me *your* name?" she asked.

"Of course. Pierre-Terrail. Pierre-Terrail Kuthan."

"Pierre-Terrail sounds French."

"My mother is French. I was named after one of her ancestors-- a military hero. Not like me." He touched her hands. They were beautiful, narrow hands. His mother had told him that it was important to look at a girl's hands. It was always the wife who set the tone in the household. "Can I see you again Lybed? On Friday they'll give me a pass to the hospital for my third typhus shot. I could be away the whole day."

"I don't know."

"Why?" Three tanks rolled past the park making a frightful One was a 60-ton Skoda belonging to a Todenkopf SS unit. ial Komsomol meeting we were told not to fraternize army because they are all rapists."

"Why then?"

"I have to write a paper for school. Pushkin's influence on Turgenev, Dostoevski, Gogol, and on contemporary Soviet writers. It's due on Monday"

"That's why you came to look at Pushkin? For inspiration?"

"No." She was giggling. "You'll think me strange if I tell you why."

"I think you strange already, but in the nicest possible way."

"I visited Pushkin for atonement."

"Like 'in propitiation for my sins'?"

"Not my sins exactly, though I have many to be pardoned for." She crossed herself in the strange Russian way, then for a moment her hands touched palm to palm in a sign of prayer.

"Lybed," he said. He felt tears in his throat that made him remember reading as an eight-year-old the story of the one-legged lead soldier in love with a paper ballerina—that part where the ballerina is blown into the fireplace and the boy searching for his toy soldier next morning finds only a lead heart buried in the ashes. He thought then that loving somebody made life painful. Nothing had changed.

"I've been paying visits to Pushkin with my grandmother since I was six years old," Lybed said. They brought flowers to atone for her family's part in Pushkin's death, she told him. Her great-great-grandfather Konstantin had been Pushkin's classmate at the Imperial Lyceum. When years later Pushkin decided to fight a duel for the honor of his wife, nobody would volunteer to be his attendant because the Tsar had outlawed dueling. Only his old classmate Konstantin, by then a lieutenant-colonel in the Imperial Army, would agree to be his second. Konstantin's dropped hat signaled the start of the duel that killed Pushkin.

"Since then," Lybed said, "it's been the duty of the women of our family to remember Pushkin. First we went to the statue in

Moscow, then when the family moved to Kiev we started visiting him here. Now that Grandmamma is old it is my duty. I am almost seventeen."

He wanted to say that on Friday he would be twenty-one, but instead he said, "Thank God."

"What are you thanking God for?"

"You and Pushkin and Madame Ivanovna. I would have never known that you existed if it wasn't for Pushkin."

"And the war," she said. "Don't forget the war."

"How could anyone forget the war?" He searched her face like a myopic who had lost his spectacles but was determined to read the message because his life depended on it. "You are beautiful."

"Only Grandmamma ever said that I was beautiful. But that's because she loved me."

He wanted to say he loved her too but instead he said: "Pushkin loved you too. '*I loved you; and perhaps I love you still,/The flame, perhaps, is not extinguished; yet/ It burns so quietly within my soul,/No longer should you feel distressed by it,/Silently and hopelessly I loved you,/At times too jealous and at times too shy...*' I am sorry. I forget the rest." He was blushing.

"'*God grant you find another who will love you/As tenderly and truthfully as I*' . . . I had to memorize it last year but I don't want to be someone's lost love."

They were looking at each other. He was thinking that he had glimpsed her soul. He wanted the whole world to know that he loved her. He took her hand and kissed it.

"Don't do that. People are looking at us," but she didn't take her hand away.

A platoon of German infantry marched by singing 'Erika'. They were passed by a very loud, drab motorcycle with a light machinegun on the deck of its sidecar.

"I have to go home now," Lybed said. "I don't want Grandmamma to start worrying about me."

"Can we meet again on Friday?"

"I don't know. Where? When?"

"At the intersection of Vladimiriskaya and Kalinin Streets at thirteen hundred hours?"

"What time is that?"

"One o'clock. After I get my typhus shot. Can you be there?"

"That's two days from now. In two days you won't remember me."

"That isn't something you should joke about."

"All right. On Friday I'll be at the intersection of Vladimiriskaya and Kalinin Streets at thirteen hundred hours. I'll take you to meet my grandmother."

They stood up. She seemed even smaller, more vulnerable surrounded by the merry-go-round of war that endlessly circled the park: tractors pulling 150mm Bofors howitzers and 80mm Anti-Aircraft guns, tanks of all sizes with their long and short-barrel canons, large gray open trucks packed with steel helmeted soldiers, pulling a mixture of Czech 37mm, Belgian 47mm and German 50mm Anti-tank guns behind them.

"They are all going in the same direction," he said.

"That's the way to Kursk. I was there to visit my other grandmother before the war started. We need to get across the street. Let's run for it." She took his hand.

* * * * * *

The 30th Tank Regiment's post included a large schoolhouse and outbuildings, housing, shops with carpentry tools and automotive equipment. There was also a huge parade ground that before the war must have been several soccer fields. Now it was

11

filled with tanks. He had arrived in the middle of an unscheduled church service. The tall, ascetic priest stood on the parade ground surrounded by the men of the regiment.

He was preaching on the possibilities and problems of human life that in their own situation came down to the simple essentials of survival.

"Yet even so we are not allowed to forget that the divine intention for us was the realization that we exist for higher ends even amidst fighting and enduring this war," he said. "Jesus sees us. This 'seeing' means much more than the way we see each other, or the way we search for our enemies to kill them before they kill us. Jesus sees us as he saw the man who had been blind since birth and could not see Him. This story is about God's transforming grace. Because Jesus sees us we are able to see Him. Saint John wrote: 'Herein is love, not that we loved God, but that he loved us, and sent his Son to be the propitiation for our sins'."

It was getting darker. Standing at the edge of the throng he shivered. The temperature had dropped several degrees. On Friday the twenty-sixth, the day after tomorrow he'd be twenty-one provided an aerial bombardment didn't kill him in the meantime or if somebody's automatic weapon didn't turn him into a many-holed Trappist cheese while he was on his way to the military hospital at the intersection of Vladimiriskaya and Kalinin Streets. Perhaps he shouldn't have asked Lybed to meet him there. It might be too dangerous. That was where Shanie Szentvari was shot by the partisans the other day. They had graduated from the National Military Academy together. Shanie had served with the 101st Towed Artillery Battalion stationed thirty kilometers from Kiev.

"We are praying in the midst of war in a place many of us never knew existed.

Death is our close companion making the crucifixion the reality of a triumphant conquest over evil in order that man might recognize the heart of God, and that God might get through to the heart of man. This is our only Redemption." The priest halted for a moment then raised his arm.

"May the almighty and merciful Lord grant us pardon, absolution and remission of our sins this night and ever more. Amen."

* * * * * *

On Thursday September the twenty-fifth at 0400 hours a general alarm sounded for the 30th Tank Regiment. HQ gave them two hours to move out. The situation in Kursk had deteriorated.

He woke up not able to think straight as if with a hangover. He had slept in his father's brown, white-dotted dressing-gown for good luck and because it gave him a sense of sophistication. It was not till he was fully dressed with his carbine in his hands listening to the tank engines being revved up that he remembered Lybed. He didn't know the name of her street, or her address, there was no way he could contact her. He only knew how to pronounce her name correctly: Lybed Osipnova Lihoded. Lybed Osipnova Lihoded. Disappearing now like a migrating bird sensing the onslaught of snow would negate even the few hours that they had spent together. She would wait for him tomorrow afternoon but by the evening he would have become a brief, sad memory of a time when the Nazis and some of their allies occupied Kiev. Her grandmother would remind her that she had already predicted this outcome but would comfort her never-the-less.

What comfort for you? Long forgotten/ Amidst the storms of new emotions,/It will not offer to your soul/Pure and tender memories.

"Lieutenant," a red-faced angry major was yelling at him. "Wake up and get on with it."

Standing in the turret of the Panzer Kampfwagen IV he inhaled the familiar, homey smells of his tank and felt the reassuring throb of the engine. This was reality. The future that did not exist couldn't hurt him. Nobody had promised him a twenty-first birthday party.

By the time they reached the park to become a part of the merry-go-round there was enough light for him to see the bench with the sawed-off back where yesterday, a lifetime ago they had sat facing each other.

But on a silent day of sorrow,/Speak my name in your grief. Just say: /There is a memory of me, there is/In the world a heart in which I live.

Tossed by the Elephants

It was on August 26 that he decided to leave Hungary, to leave behind everything that mattered in his life, to escape. The decision was made dispassionately with a clear knowledge of the consequences. Death at the hands of the border guards wouldn't be worse than the dull pain brought on by the constant daily humiliations that focused his mind on what his life had become under the new regime that wasn't even new anymore, and the clear realization of what he had lost. For a relatively long time now he had clung to the remnant that resembled and sometimes even imitated his old life but he could lie to himself only for so long without taking part in his own mutilation, turning himself into a fly in an experimental fruit jar demonstrating the psychological truth of "premature cognitive commitment," that exposure to a limited horizon for an extended period would turn that horizon into a perceived reality. Beyond the barbed-wire-topped fences there

15

was nothing. It was no good thinking further than that. The Communist Party intellectuals wrote (they were the only ones who were allowed to write anything), that the old myth that God was a God of history who had intersected it in the form of the least powerful, a human baby, was even more stupid, more hopeless than throwing salt over one's shoulder for good luck. There was no need to understand dialectical materialism to be able to observe reality as opposed to old wives' tale: it was a scientific-historical fact that the future belonged to Marxism-Leninism. The regime was all-powerful; it rewarded its loyal servants and punished its foes. To dispute this proved one's backwardness. It was also considered treason. He had to get out.

The clouds were big, white eiderdowns on August 26th. He was sitting at a small, square, marble-topped table outside the Saint Gellert Hotel restaurant drinking a double-double espresso when he made his decision. Saint Gellert had been one of Budapest's premier hotels before World War II but it was run-down now like everything else in this city of bullet holes and shored-up houses. It overlooked the Danube toward the wharves, church spires, and the still imposing parliament building on the Pest side. The closest bridge to the hotel used to be called Ferenc Jozsef Bridge named for the Austro-Hungarian emperor Franz Josef. The retreating German Army had blown it up just as they had blown up all of Budapest's bridges. After rebuilding, the Communists renamed it Freedom Bridge. The ribbon-cutting ceremony was conducted by Minister Gero, the worst sadist in the Communist hierarchy. He had interviewed Minister Gero and had written a flattering article about "Bridge Builder Gero" for the Soviet Army's Hungarian-language newspaper which had hired him when no other paper would because he had been a tank commander in the Hungarian Army. It wasn't too difficult to write the article: his monthly salary of 25 kilos of beans, 25 kilos of potatoes, 10 kilos of flour, and ½ kilo of lard had kept his family functioning in the short haul when inflation had reached the stage where the price of a streetcar ticket that had cost a million pengos in the morning would double by the evening. His brother-in-law, a brain surgeon was told that he would be allowed to bring his wife and mother-in-law to the clinic to be fed also, twice a day beginning in September.

Sitting at the table, looking up to his left he could see the grey rocks of Gellert Hill that had formed the cave that used to house what was commonly called the Rock Chapel, his mother's favorite place of prayer. The entrance to the chapel had been sealed with cement by the Hungarian Communist government.

In the summer of 1944, the year the Nazis took over Hungary, he was home on leave from the Eastern Front and he had made a lunch date with his mother at the Saint Gellert Hotel. An air raid delayed him on the Pest side of the Danube and by the time he had crossed Ferenc Jozsef Bridge he was half an hour late. There had been a direct hit on the restaurant. It was cordoned off by firefighting apparatus and hastily erected barricades. He had stood there smelling the burning wood and something else that he tried not to identify, something that had haunted his dreams and his waking hours, a smell that had impregnated his olfactory nerves and thus made the existence of the horror of the scorched bodies of tank crews a permanent reality. He turned and began to walk up to the chapel. There was no need to run. He walked slowly like a fearful cardiac patient. One of the policemen had told him that everybody in the restaurant had burned to death. The firemen were only trying to contain the flames.

In the chapel candles were grouped like beds of silver flowers; the candlelight wavering with the moving air swept the lower part of the cave's ceiling then disappeared into the high, dark spaces that reached into infinity where hope bundled in black draperies slowly suffocated. He was looking for the image of Mary, Mother of God, whom his own mother used to ask for prayers now and in the hour of her death. Mary was there to his right presiding over one of the banks of candles her white dress and golden crown gleaming, the Babe safe in the crook of her arm. He kept his eyes on her as if doing so would cause the falling bombs, the fires, death, his own fear, and despair to disappear as if the air raid sirens had never sounded their cry and the War that had already killed his father had never been started. He knelt down, his hands squeezing each other in a mute appeal asking for the restoration of their lives. It was then that he heard someone praying in French. His mother always prayed in French, the French of her girlhood, the language of the lycee, the language of the nuns.

"Mother!" She was kneeling with her eyes closed praying for him, praying for the souls of the departed. "Mother."

* * * * * *

The senseless cruelties like the sealing of the chapel had come with the local party leaders' taking over from the Red Army. He had been ordered to a police station with no reason given. Waiting in the station house, sitting on a bench coated with dirt that gave the old varnish underneath the appearance of having been scorched, he could hear a clock relentlessly counting down the seconds toward his turn when he would be told once again if he would live or die. Mingled with the stale, cigarette smoke he could smell fear, his own and that of the others, men and women who were waiting with him. He used to think that with the ending of the war, pain, hunger, fear, and hate would vanish but he knew now that he had survived only to have new torture thrust on him. He had no future with a regime whose intellectuals' professed ideology, the love of mankind, was only an antidote to individual love that interfered with the breaking of eggs so necessary in the making of Utopian omelets. The state had become a god that Molech-like consumed its children. Its prophet, kept under glass like a piece of dried-out cheese, was shown to the masses in a quasi-religious ceremony acolyted by goose-stepping soldiers.

After five hours' waiting at the police station he was told to go home and report to his block leader once a week. He knew then that there was no hope for a reprieve for his sin of having been born. If he wanted to live he had to escape his country that, surrounded by barbed-wire-topped fences with plowed free-fire zones planted with mines, had become a gigantic jail.

* * * * * *

It was raining on the morning of September 17, the day he was to leave. The rain splashing on the river made tribal tattoo marks on the water. He was looking across the Danube at the empty, white stone building next to the sealed chapel on Gellert Hill that used to belong to the Paulist Fathers. Like Henry the VIII, the Communist Party dissolved the religious orders and confiscated their properties. Carrying the politics of envy to its logical conclusion, most of the rooms in their apartment had been confiscated, (he and his mother were allowed to keep what used to be cook's quarters), and were filled with four families from the outlying districts. These were the people who enjoyed marking seventeenth century landscapes, family portraits, even a Murillo Madonna with beards, mustachios and sickle & hammer symbols. In short time the Persian carpets and the whole apartment smelled like the strangers.

On the river an unseen tugboat hooted, sounding like the desperate cry of the last of a dying species but then an answer came and a string of barges hove into sight looking like a Morse code message printed on muddy-green paper telling him to move, to get on with it. There really was no choice if he wanted to have a quality of life beyond mere survival. He turned away from the window, picked up an old canvas suitcase with leather reinforced edges that contained two pairs of socks, three pairs of underpants, five monogrammed silk shirts, his old military academy winter tunic, a regular army officer's summer tunic, a toothbrush, a copy of Dickens' David Copperfield in German translation and left the room. The kitchen smelled like the wolves' cage in the zoo. He had managed for months not to notice it or the women who were already squabbling, their faces the color of yellowish winter apples, distorted either by anger or tears.

Out on the street he felt as if he had jumped a first hurdle that forever severed his connection with the apartment, his home once that had become purgatory, a foretaste of hell that waited for him if he insisted on staying in his allotted room, a situation that diminished him, that forced him to be less than human. He couldn't tell even his own mother for both of their sakes that he was leaving.

The rain blowing in from the river blinded him and he stumbled on the sidewalk as if he were a horse in training for the jumps, miscounting its steps over the caveletti laid out on the ground. He had a long way to go. He began to run.

* * * * * *

The long-distance buses started from Moricz Zsigmond Square, off Bartok Bela Road on the Buda side. There was romance about these buses with their throbbing diesel engines and shiny bodies that allowed a lucky few with hard currency and connections to high Party officials to leave the country with valid passports that made it possible for them to go beyond the Soviet zone in Austria to reach the French, English or even the US sector in Salzburg and never return; but most of the people on the bus were only going to some western towns of Hungary where the bus stopped on its way to the Austro-Hungarian border and Vienna.

At 9:30 the man in the brown leather coat and brown hat standing next to the driver's seat gave the passengers a last, hard look and left. The door closed, the air brakes sighed and the bus began to move, bouncing and splashing through the rainwater-filled potholes. Sitting almost over the back wheels he thought he should be posting in rhythm with the bumping bus if he wanted to keep his backbone from crumbling. The family had always traveled to Vienna by rail in their own carriage that allowed the more important household staff and pets to go with them. As a boy he was always embarrassed when people at the station were looking at them, the servants directing the porters with the luggage, Cook carrying his sister's canary in a draped cage, the dogs pulling at their leashes, Nanny shooing the children as if they were geese, all following their mother outside— their father would be driven by car to join them later— toward the waiting fleet of cabs.

Bartok Bela Road was paved with cobblestones that made the bus tires sing a different tune, a lullaby that made him sleepy and allowed him to stop saying good-by to all the passing statues of statesmen, generals, revolutionary heroes and poets.

* * * * * *

He had to get off the bus fifty kilometers from the Hungarian-Austrian border. Strangers who went any closer were taken to the police station for interrogation. The bus had gone in a cloud of dust leaving him in the small town he had known for only three days having been billeted here during the war. He headed for the only building that retained its charm and dignity in this town—an overgrown village really—that had lost its beauty when all the thatched-roofed, whitewashed adobe farm-houses were pulled down to make room for the ugly, square, plastered-brick villas and the five- and six-story prefab, 'socialist' apartment buildings. The Reformed church was a triumph of folk art. Its carved doors, pews, pulpit, and the Lord's Table reflected the builders' Transylvanian origin. He remembered reading a printed note at the entrance that explained that the church had been built after World War I by refugees who had settled here after Transylvania was ceded to the Romanians in the early twenties.

Walking on the street with a suitcase in hand made him conspicuous enough to expect the police to hail him. Because he had been ordered to report once a week to his block leader he was not supposed to leave Budapest. Even the suspicion that he was trying to leave the country would earn him five to fifteen years' hard labor. He entered the church and closed the door behind him. The light coming through the windowpanes poured on the lectern supporting a Bible as if to define the focus in this house of God, then the light withdrew and the dancing motes ceased to be. He felt overcome with longing for something or somebody beyond the spatiotemporal that he could not name. It left him in a momentary cocoon of silence, a sanctuary of peace that was shattered by the flinging open of the church door and he was hit by a rifle-butt. He was lying on the stone floor, surrounded by the blue epauletted security police who were ransacking his suitcase. One of them found his copy of David Copperfield and was using it to beat his head. Rifle-butts were pounding his feet and back. He was sinking further and further into the depths of pain thinking that he was no more than self-deluding Mr. Micawber tossed by the elephants. In his despair he cried out to God. Without Him his life and death had no more meaning than the trampled down grass in front of the church.

* * * * * *

When he was able to walk again, he was charged with anti-state activities and sentenced to 10 years in the Recsk concentration camp.

Stress Test

It was six o'clock in the morning, still dark. North Florida Regional Medical Center liked to start their "procedures" early. The headlights illuminated the frozen English peas turning them into dangling silver ropes and their vegetable garden itself into a backstage jumble. The first frost had hit just before Christmas, early by north Florida standards, but most of the winter vegetables had survived.

He drove up onto their blacktop road and turned left. To his right, in the distance, he could see a lighter, narrow band as if he had pulled up the shade a bit to peer outside. Gainesville was fifteen miles away.

The road dipped, running between the woods. In winter the deer came over from the San Felasco State Park to graze the ryegrass he and his son planted for their horses. They were there now in the bend of the road, five of them, their heads held up haughtily like bewitched princesses. Eyes gleaming they executed a series of grand jetes, flying toward the fence then over it into their wild life refuge.

The squirrels, already croaking their love songs, chased each other, dashing madly across the road without looking in either direction. He resolved to talk to his grandchildren about road safety. He drove around the big oak tree that stood in the middle of the road like a sentinel and stopped before turning onto county road 241.

He felt his heart beginning to fibrillate again. The second prescription had not worked either.

He thought of the young whippoorwill his dogs had nosed out from its nest on top of a clump of grass. Picking up the bird he had felt the rapid heartbeats turning arrhythmic. There were no wound marks on the bird, no blood on the feathers, but the bird died and he had yelled at the dogs because he couldn't do anything else.

A week after the death of the whippoorwill he was sitting in his doctor's examining room having come for a routine checkup. He was waiting for the sound of the doctor removing his chart from the slot in the door then the pause as he glanced at it before entering the room. He was always tense sitting in the cell-like examining rooms even though he had been in America over 40 years.

When the sound came he knew that they were coming in to get him. Then he was back in the interrogation room, hogtied, a broom handle thrust behind his knees and across his arms cutting off his circulation.

He was watching a small man kicking him with the regularity of a pendulum but not feeling anything. The only sound he heard was his own heart out of sync with the pendulum and he hoped that this time

26

he would be allowed to step over the line for good because this couldn't go on and on.

"Are you all right?"

It was Alan, his doctor and friend. Alan was his son's age, a small man like that other one. There was a symmetry here that he should understand, two sides of a coin that had something to do with classical Greek philosophy. He was a bit dizzy.

"Let's get you up on the table."

* * * * * *

He drove across an Interstate 75 overpass. The early morning fog made the semis swim in a white current below him, festive whales adorned for Christmas, then the road descended, turning in a wide sweep, and his headlights picked out the gravestones in Mount Nebo's churchyard and the cows in the next pasture scattered like prehistoric monoliths.

He turned on the radio. It was set to the PBS station because he liked classical music and disliked the intrusion of commercials but it seemed that whenever he was driving the news was on. The local segment was still full of speculations about the gruesome murders of four university students. The interviews with people who couldn't possibly help solve this heinous crime created a circus-like atmosphere made indecent by the thought that the parents, relatives and friends of the victims might be listening.

The national broadcast wasn't any better. People holding opposing views were snarling at each other as if their aim was not to offer mutual help in solving national problems but to wrest power through character assassination.

Christmas, now two weeks past, had been mentioned only as a statistic of the Retail Merchants Association. God, who in the past had been confessed on some coins and government buildings

27

to be trustworthy, could be glimpsed only through the rantings of media preachers wanting to establish their own Disneyland.

He turned off the radio. It had made him feel like an alien, a stranger here. Not that he was longing for the country he had fled after World War II. With the existence of glasnost and perestroika he had the opportunity now to return if he wanted to. It wasn't that. He longed for a country of his own, where Christians weren't ridiculed on university campuses as superstitious Yahoos because they loved God, where his brethren would not be characterized in mainstream literature, in films and on TV shows as narrow, hypocritical, money-grubbing people whose intellectual integrity was always suspect.

Just before Christmas he had been invited to the circumcision of Alan's younger son. The mohel, who was also a rabbi, told the gathered community and friends of the family that circumcision was not a hygienic measure but a symbol of the covenant between God and His people, a witness to an act that was initiated by God, not man.

He had stood there with the others, a friendly stranger, hearing the child mewing in pain but also hearing Isaiah: "Here am I, and the children the Lord has given me. We are signs and symbols..."

He turned onto the scenic drive that was part of San Felasco State Park, feeling his heart shudder like a car's engine with electrical trouble. He didn't really mind. Like the Magi he was traveling west but always looking east.

* * * * * *

His headache got worse in the Medical Center's waiting room. He was hungry and needed a cup of coffee.

28

It reminded him of the war when he had always waited for something to happen, for the food or the gasoline or some spare parts and ammunition to catch up with them or a bombardment to stop or the snow to melt or waited for somebody so high up that he had never even laid eyes on him to make a decision that could land him in a prison camp for years or maim him for life or kill him.

For distraction he picked up a magazine and looked at pictures of people whom he didn't know but who seemed familiar, as if they had all come out of the same handsome mold with only shadings to differentiate between them. What made it unlike a family photo album was that instead of brief captions there was detailed text that revealed intimate tidbits about their love lives, marriages, and divorces.

Reading the magazine made him feel like a Peeping Tom. He had always wanted to be a normal American but had been taught at an early age that one entertained guests in one's public rooms not in one's bedroom and early training was hard to unlearn.

His heart was beating steadily. Perhaps he didn't really need the stress test. Insurance wouldn't pay the whole amount and his wife always worried about money. Thirty-eight years ago he had been a $90-a-month ranch hand and they had lived with their baby daughter in a one-room shanty. It had made his wife insecure forever.

* * * * * *

He was lying on a trolley half naked, with electrodes attached to his chest, facing a big blinking machine that reminded him of the UNIVACs on TV on election nights. The room was chilly, like airports used to be before oil became too expensive. He felt the same excitement and anticipation he used to feel before boarding ships and later planes for overseas passages.

Actually it was more like his coming to a new country, his coming to America in 1950, a husband of three months, on the SS United States, a ship partly converted back from troopship to civilian use.

All he had seen of America in the newsreels was the New York waterfront with the Statue of Liberty and the strange bald mountains in the western movies. Much later he realized that there wasn't a frame big enough to hold what the United States of America was, not just as a geographical entity but as an idea. He had to see the Grand Canyon to realize this and to worry about his wife and children at the edge of this immensity that could not be captured in its entirety by the powers of art or any optical device.

This was also true of the Far Country he barely knew beyond a few short descriptions that had excited his imagination with its endless possibilities.

It was then that for the first time he thought of the husk he must leave behind which the people he loved would have to deal with. He was 6'1", 211 lbs. Dead weight, it was more than four feed sacks that only his son could handle but not if he was away on a business trip.

What if Kate, who had told him just the other day that she wasn't four-and-a-half anymore but would be five in April, came to help in the vegetable garden and saw her grandfather lying there like a pile of discarded tires?

What if John Gray walked through the woods with his Mummy to visit Grandfadoux?

He had read somewhere that more times than not people knew that a heart attack was imminent. He would have time to walk down to the barn to die out of sight on the cement walkway or in one of the stalls and start his journey soaring silently as in his dream flights toward a blue sky dotted with fluffy clouds like fat white pillows piled up on village beds.

The technician came back and inserted a needle into his arm. This was the nuclear medicine part.

It was three o'clock in the afternoon by the time he left North Florida Regional Medical Center, feeling as if he had been left behind on the pier with his packed bags.

He was not going to die. His heart was not diseased. It could pump a bit stronger than it did but that could be corrected with medication. There was no explanation for the fibrillation. It just happened sometimes.

He drove up onto Interstate 75. It was the fastest way home from the Medical Center. The weather had turned balmy, the air smelled as if February had suddenly decided to become Spring; the roadside woods were dotted with the lacy-white flowers of wild plum trees.

Cars with out-of-state license plates whizzed by, tourists on their way home. Some, like the car with the Quebec license, had a long way to go, but even cars from Georgia were speeding. He was a tourist too, even if he got off at Alachua, the third exit. It didn't make sense for him to speed, especially not in this car with 175,000 on the odometer.

That was another thing; he'd have to buy a car now and not leave it to his son to choose one for his mother.

He got off Interstate 75, turned left, drove over it on the overpass, then down the steep hill past a Shell station that had become more and more grungy since a Jiffy store with its super pumps had opened on the other side of the overpass.

The road climbed and he looked left to catch a glimpse of the miniature horses but they were gone for good. The farm had become an "estate" with an immense art deco entrance that reminded him of the old Budapest zoo entrance. Across from it the "Female Protective Society" church had prospered materially judging from its sign that was in two colors now: yellow and green. He still hadn't seen anybody entering or leaving it as if the long, white frame building in the middle of the neatly cut lawn was lying in a permanent accouchement. Five hundred yards past it the 7 & 11 store had been turned into a 19th century brick fort with iron barred windows and doors. The glass parts of its gasoline pumps had been shattered.

At the stop sign he turned right onto County Road 241. Kelly training stables were doing well. Their rink had been repainted this year.

Next to it, the Baptists had added a brick facade to the front of the steel building that served as their sanctuary. The same love of God that built Chartres Cathedral had placed this steel structure—manufactured to store feed and fertilizer—in the middle of a wooded lot and surrounded it with flowering bushes. The azaleas were a mix of pleasing lavenders and pinks as if nature itself had joined in the enterprise to transform the ugly lines.

He knew that this miracle of devotion would not be reported on TV, radio or in the papers—there would be a better chance if it had happened on a Jugoslav mountainside or in a little, out-of-the-way Mexican village—but this was America too, halleluiah, his home where he would be settling back down for a while.

Further down the road, on what used to be a huge pasture, he saw that the pine seedlings had overcome the pasture-grasses and weeds and were marching like little green soldiers toward the road. He drove across another Interstate 75 overpass where under him the tourists and the trucks rushed in both directions and turned into their low brick entrance-way.

Risen Indeed

Sitting behind his desk, he could see only the top of the palm tree that grew in the courtyard at the corner of Killion Hall, the fronds waving with the exaggerated coquetry of geisha fans in a Gilbert and Sullivan operetta. The telephone receiver, his ancient, implacable foe, was pressing against his ear. He was listening to Corrine Young. He knew her from vestry meetings as a calm, middle-aged woman. She sounded distraught now, as if she were speaking from a sinking ship or reading the last communication of a lost revolution before the radio station shut down. Somebody had sent her a church publication from New Jersey in which the bishop discussed his visit to a Buddhist temple and his prayer before a Buddhist shrine. "I am not a Buddhist and do not expect to become one," the bishop wrote. "I do not believe, however, that the God I worship has been captured solely in my words, my forms, or my concepts." He had experienced only "a Western

Christ, an American Christ, a major force in behavior control in the Western world and thus a source of guilt that played such a large part in the Western psyche." He had never met the universal Christ, the risen Christ. Since Christianity was only one of many equally valid world religions, there should be no more going into the world to preach the good news to all creation. The bishop of Newark rescinded the Great Commission. Once again, he thought, Christ crucified was a foolishness and a stumbling block to someone.

"You're not listening," Corrine said.

"I am." Below him the courtyard was silent and clean. He wanted peace, palpable now with the students on their Easter vacation. The telephone cord kept him prisoner.

"Can you imagine Buddhists embarrassed by Buddhism's 'exclusiveness'?" she said.

After the death of her alcoholic husband six years ago, Corrine had gone back to school to get a degree in comparative religions.

"Can you imagine them standing in St. Michael's nave?"

He could. He could imagine a fat Buddha appearing after the announcements, after the little children had come in from Sunday school to join their parents in the Eucharist. The Buddha could sit where Santa Claus usually stood on Saint Nicholas' Day.

With a great clatter, two boys on skateboards bounced down the steps in front of Dobson Hall, the humanities building, then with a loud thud landed in the courtyard. One of them looked up. Skateboards were prohibited in the buildings and courtyards. He waved. The boys waved back.

"What hurts me most," Corrine said, "is that the bishop deliberately wounds us by calling the Resurrection 'physical resuscitation' when he is so sensitive and understanding of everybody else's feelings. He knows exactly the words to use to hurt us most. Why does he do it?"

34

"To prod us into bellowing nasty and stupid things." He remembered the electric cattle prods the buyers brought to the ranch, the bellowing, terrified cows, the sweet smell of their sweat mixed with the smell of dust and manure. He had been a ranch hand when he first came to America.

"Without the Resurrection I have nothing," Corrine said. "You can't imagine the desolation I feel."

* * * * * *

He had reached Salzburg at five the morning in early April 1947. He was dizzy with hunger. He didn't know what day it was, but he was certain of the time. There were church clocks everywhere. By eleven, he stood on the sidewalk across from the U.S. Military Headquarters watching soldiers going in and out, all dressed in clean, well-pressed uniforms. A detachment of tall military police in shiny helmets glided on rubber-soled boots toward the barrier, demigods returning to Olympus. He had never before encountered marching soldiers without first hearing their hob-nailed boots. Two years before, in '45, Salzburg had become part of the U.S. zone. In the distant past it had been a Roman settlement named Juvavum, marked in history by the fact that it was here that Heruli had martyred Saint Maximus. After that came the Goths, Huns, and Charlemagne. When salt was found under the hills, the natives renamed the town Salzburg. From where he was standing he could see the house in which Paracelsus the alchemist had tried to turn lead into gold in the 16th century. The house, painted bluish-grey, was streaked with water marks that made it shabby and scuffed like an old boot. He watched the civilians entering the American Express offices. He decided to hit a civilian instead of a soldier. It would still land him in jail, and he had heard it on good authority in Vienna that

35

American prison food was first class. They even had plates divided into sections. In one section there would be sliced Spam, in the next beets, and the third would hold green beans.

He had seen his first American in Vienna last year after his escape from Hungary. In Vienna he had lived in the international zone, and had gone every day to the American Library on Kartner Strasse to look in the slick magazines for the beautiful pictures of food. He liked the Spam advertisement best. In the picture the tin can was partly peeled back, the remaining lower, narrower part forming a pedestal for the naked Spam. It made him think of the rotating pedestal at the nightclub CASINO ORIENTAL, on which he stood three nights a week as THE LIVING CLASSICAL STATUE, striking well-known poses to the accompaniment of classical music. He was covered with either white or bronze paint that clogged his pores and had to be removed after 25 minutes. He lived at the Hotel Wandl, because the management didn't insist on passports. The hotel was a few blocks from St. Stephan's cathedral, just off the Graben, in the international zone, where the MP's of the four occupying powers rotated every three months. When he found out that the Russians' turn was coming, he knew it was time to leave. The Russians were known to make political refugees disappear from the streets, never to be seen again. He decided to go to Salzburg, to the U.S. zone, and spent his last Napoleon gold pieces on a high-quality false passport. The passport turned out to be useless. At the final checkpoint before the U.S. sector, Russian soldiers pulled him off the Arlberg Express and marched him away from the train with a burp gun pressed into his back. At first he couldn't think at all or feel fear or any of the emotions he had expected to feel. There was nothing other than the sensation of his legs moving without his consent. The gun that touched his back had become a control rod taking over his life. He smelled the Russians: their filthy uniforms, their cigarettes (mahorka rolled in newsprint), their cooking. Their voices made him shudder: nobody had ever addressed him in Russian without abuse, as if charity and love had been expurgated from the language of Dostoevski, Tolstoi, Chekhov, Turgenev, and all the nameless, martyred saints who, for centuries, praised God extravagantly in Russian. They took him to a dirty-white farmhouse with barred windows and locked him in a large room. There were people lying all over the floor like so many abandoned bundles and suitcases left behind on a station's platform. It was almost a year since he had crossed the Hungarian-Austrian border, had crossed over fences, felt his way around land mines. He began yelling and kicking the solid door, which opened suddenly. He smelled onions, booze, and nicotine. A bowlegged little Mongol in a greasy uniform was standing in the opening, waving his submachine gun as if trying to shoo chickens with a broom. To his amazement, he heard himself laugh because he was thinking that his own ancestors must have looked like this in the 13th century when they were fleeing from Genghis Khan to a walled town in Hungary. He took the gun, twisting it away by its round magazine. Then he heard a sound that was like a watermelon splitting open and he was standing alone. The others watched him walk through the open doorway.

The clock on Salzburg cathedral boomed out the quarter hour. Another clock on another church steeple boomed a second later, swelling the sound; then another joined their combined echo till the last one whirred all alone with the sick, dry sound of a clockwork in a child's abused toy. He looked up at the Monschberg, at the fort crowning its summit surrounded by snowcapped mountains. A young man, wearing ski boots, ski pants, and a Norwegian pullover, came through the door of the American Express office, putting bills into his wallet. He followed him, rehearsing his own moves. It was very simple. He would hit the American and people would call the MP's, stationed right here. He would be taken to their jail to eat off a divided plate. First the slices of Spam. . . . He was only two steps behind him when the man turned and looked back. He had a friendly face that smiled at the world in general, even smiled at him. He couldn't hit him.

By nighttime he didn't feel hunger pains anymore, only light-headedness that made his eyes heavy and made him think of himself as a rundown gramophone emitting unintended comic sounds. He needed to lie down to stop the burning in his back, but he had no money for a hotel. The train station was out of the question. The police checked for tickets and identity papers. If they wanted to they could put him back into the Russian zone. The wet sidewalk turned icy gleamed in the glare of the streetlights. The wind blew down from Monschberg shaking the leaf-less trees, shaking him. The cathedral clock began to strike the hour, counting up slowly so that the other clocks could catch up. He crossed the square and entered the cathedral by a side door. It was already warmer inside the vestibule. He opened the second door. He had expected to see streetlights filtered through the stained glass he remembered from before the war when he had been his mother's companion at the Mozart Festivals, but the stained glass had been replaced by clear glass and he was surrounded by light he remembered reflecting from the snow before the machine guns opened up and he had watched people around him dance in a strange, contemporary ballet, bending their limbs at impossible angles before they whirled away to create a mediaeval tableau on the red snow.

He tried to find the ruby glow that should have been there to guide him toward the altar but the lamp was not lit. The altar was bare. It had been stripped of its linen and candlesticks. The door of the safe behind the altar was open. It was empty like the Parthenon was empty, always had been empty. He was standing in empty space where the sound of weeping and crying would always be heard, where hope had ceased forever. There would never be a new heaven and new earth, a new Jerusalem. He cried with dry sobs as if he had been drained even of his tears. He cried for the empty world, he cried for himself, he cried for his little Mongol great-great grandfather.

* * * * * *

The palm fronds stretching toward his window imitated the hands of a narcissistic model in a press-on nail advertisement, then the March wind transformed the vain hands into the beseeching hands of a drowning person. The courtyard was empty and silent after the departure of the boys with their skateboards. He decided to go home early. It was Maundy Thursday. They would be going to the 7:30 service. His wife had also signed them up for the 3 a.m. to 4 a.m. Good Friday vigil.

The streetlight coming through the rose window was the only illumination in the church. The Roberts, the couple they came to relieve, passed them in silence on their way out. The stained glass in the rose window was an abstract design, the dominating reddish-brown color like simmering blood about to come to a boil. By a trick of light or perspective, the image of Christ the King which was suspended from the ceiling appeared to be in the middle of the boiling cauldron. Last night with the lights on at the 7:30 Maundy Thursday service the rose window had been a jeweled backdrop to the image of Christ the King. The service had begun with foot-washing and had ended with the dismantling of the altar and the extinguishing of the sanctuary lamp. There was no recessional. People simply got up and silently left.

Nobody stopped to talk. Outside he had been surprised to see the lit-up neon signs of the shops and fast food places and hear the muted bells as cars drove in and out of service stations as if nothing was about to happen.

He knelt down beside his wife in the first pew. He was feeling dizzy. His stomach possessed an independent intelligence that automatically switched on if he was awakened between 2 and 4 a.m., as if between these parameters he had been programmed at some cataclysmic occasion to feel fear. He noticed the prayer books left open for them at the appropriate page and also literature for meditation. It irritated him, just as he was irritated with people who underlined books. He closed his eyes.

He saw his three-year-old granddaughter dressed in a white jogging suit standing with her back to him on a scroll of white clouds and blue sky. She turned and smiled at him. It wasn't his granddaughter, but it was the same smile: teeth even and white, chocolate-brown eyes sparkling. He felt incredible happiness, wholeness, then without warning the child vanished and he saw the soccer fields at his school where, toward the end of the war, the goalposts had been transformed into gibbets. He saw the people again with the boards around their necks, their heads bent, hanging next to each other, moving slowly like pendulums in some monstrous clock. He was a pendulum. He was part of the clock. There was no way to escape.

* * * * * *

The smell was a mixture of the Easter lilies on the altar, the wildflowers the children had arranged on a wire frame in the shape of a cross, and the lingering odor of incense from the swinging incense carried in the procession. The daylight coming through the rose window reflected from the fair linen, silver

40

chalice, and ciborium on the altar, and the festive garments of the attending priests, deacons, lay readers, and acolytes. The servers moved as in a slow dance, feeding the people kneeling at the altar rail. Corrine Young was among them. They all lived in an antagonistic world that hated and wounded them constantly with ridicule and hostility reserved exclusively for them that for some reason was perceived as sophistication or even as art.

The line moved closer to the altar. He and his wife were among the last. The ushers were right behind them. Some of the white-robed acolytes smiled at him. He had known many of them since they were babes-in-arms, had seen them at their baptisms. He was home here, home where he was loved with a particular love that went beyond his understanding, that could turn a wooden-tongued stranger into a son. He knelt down and made a cross out of his hands.

"The Body of our Lord Jesus Christ keep you in ever-lasting life," the server said, pressing the wafer into the palm of his hand.

Like a horseshoe the wooden railing encircled the altar. He was one of the people who had sanded it in '68 when they had built the sanctuary. From where he was kneeling he could look across at some of the other communicants. Their faces were radiant, glowing with an inner light that was unearthly in its beauty.

"The Blood of our Lord Jesus Christ keep you in everlasting life."

He drank, then stood up and followed his wife back to their pew. A solo trumpet began to play Charles Wesley's "Jesus Christ Is Risen Today." Because it was Easter he looked up at the choir loft where his young friend Michael used to play his silver Bach Stradivarius, lifting the whole church heavenward. Michael's trumpet had sounded soft and tender, as if he were incapable of uttering harsh sounds, and there was sometimes a forlorn tone that seemed out of character. He had known Michael since he was nine years old. He knew the whole family. The trumpet player wasn't Michael. Michael was dead, had died at the age of 20, and nothing he could do or say would bring him back into the choir loft this Easter or any other. He couldn't stop himself from crying. He wondered if he should leave now, stop disturbing people, go outside. Then his name was called and he recognized the voice as all the others who had been called had recognized it. It was the voice of Him Who cooked fish on a charcoal fire for his friends and said: "Come and have breakfast." It was the voice that made them know that beyond chronos was the kairos of everlasting life. He looked at the image of Christ the King, at the Easter lilies on the altar, at the cross made of wildflowers, and he cried out with the instinctive cry of the newborn.

"Christ is risen. Christ is risen."

"Risen indeed," the others shouted back.

Verity Unseen

He was standing next to the small bedroom window where he could look down on the Devonshire coastline. The bedroom had been a stable hayloft for more than a hundred years before his in-laws converted it for their Florida family's two-year stay. It was a simple conversion: the floor had been vacuumed, two wardrobes, a desk for his typewriter, a bunk bed and a double mattress had been installed through the trapdoor. There was also a wooden display case housing grandfather's bird-egg and butterfly collections nailed to the wall close to the children's bunk bed. He and Meg slept on the double mattress placed on the floor under a skylight set into the sloping roof framing the branches of a cherry tree. The chamber pot sat discreetly under his desk. Due to the peculiarities of the British tax system installing a WC in the cottage would have brought heavy new taxes. Fortunately, there was a conveniently located outside WC twenty yards on the east side of his in-laws two story stone house, The Croft (a misnomer: it was a Victorian mansion not a West Highland cottage), built on a terrace surrounded on three sides by grassy banks. In front of the house a steep dell led down to a stone wall. The Croft could easily have accommodated them all but it was decided after long trans-Atlantic discussions between Meg and her parents that he, Meg and the children should have their own private space. This decision was responsible for his in-laws' turning part of the stable into a cottage. In addition to the hayloft bedroom, there was a small room downstairs with a fireplace that had been used by coachmen in the past. A sink and a hotplate had been added. They ate their suppers here and performed their light ablutions in the mornings. When it got too cold to work upstairs under the un-insulated roof, he wrote here at the table with his back to the fireplace. Once the children had left to walk down to the village school and Meg had driven off to the hospital in Exeter for her anatomy studies, the room was absolutely quiet. Sometimes he felt lonely and homesick for North Florida. But they were in England for several important reasons: Meg was completing advanced studies in Occupational Therapy that would qualify her for a position as clinical director in the U.S., and the children were getting to know their English grandparents better. But the most important reason was the possibility that his mother might be allowed out from communist Hungary to visit them in England though for some reason a visit to the US was out of the question.

In the evenings he never felt lonely or homesick. They read aloud from books Meg and her sisters had heard as children, then the hot-water bottles were filled, burped, and the stoppers secured. Everybody changed into pajamas in front of the fireplace, the fire was banked for the night and the light-switch for upstairs was clicked on. As the father it was his duty to race up the stepladder first, hold open the trapdoor while the rest of them made their charges into the icy interior of the bedroom shouting and admiring their cloudy breaths.

Perching on the edge of his desk looking through the small window of their bedroom he watched the white spumes arching over the top of the cliff like giant apparitions. Even with the window closed he could hear the shingle rolling on the beach and the cry of the seagulls. He was shivering. In seven months he still had not learned that in the English countryside unless one lived in a small cozy cottage down in the village, one had to dress warmly for the inside as well. When they had arrived on Sibet's eighth birthday on September 17th, it was a warm, sunny day. The *Flanders,* on her way to France, did not dock in England. She only dropped anchor to await a tender coming out from Plymouth. Standing on the deck of the *Flanders* surrounded by their luggage they spotted Meg's father on the approaching tender wearing his clerical collar under a light tweed jacket. Only his family called him "Father". To his small country congregations he was Mr. Wilkinson, or Wilkie. He was "broad-church." His cousin Ronald (the children's beloved Uncle Ronald), the rector of Saint Saviour in London, was an Anglo-Catholic and his congregation always addressed him as "Father". Saint Saviour was one of the few structures on East India Dock Road that remained standing after the Blitz. It was Uncle Ronald who had introduced the children to Kipling's *Just So Stories.*

Today it was too cold to try to write upstairs. He went down the steps and carefully closed the trapdoor behind him. The coal in the fireplace was alive, pulsating with the regularity of a heartbeat. He sat down at the table feeling the heat embrace his whole body. With his back to the fire he could only see the sink and the towel rack. When it was still possible to write upstairs without freezing, instead of working on the novel (for which he had received an advance), he wrote variations on the view framed by his small window. There were the grass-topped chalk hills with sheer flint-embedded sides that resembled halved sticky-buns. And sheep, puffs of white and gray clouds in the folds between the hills. Intermittently he could hear them bleating but only when the shingle on the beach, that rattled with the manic ferocity of giants shaking their dice cups, was silent for a few seconds between waves. Watching the sheep graze he noticed the lower parts of their legs were hidden in the long grass and realized what great observers the prehistoric cave painters were when in some of their paintings they didn't depict the lower legs of a deer or a horse.

He missed the horses and hoped that the young couple they had left in charge was looking after everything properly. The horses had been part of his life for the past twelve years in North Florida where many of the hunter-jumpers, show jumpers and dressage horses were bred and trained by part-time farmers like him. During those years, other than in his speech, he had become not only a generic American citizen but a southerner. When rummaging in his father-in-law's theological library the other day for something to read, he had picked *Early Church History to A.D. 313* by Henry Melvill Gwatkin, solely on the strength of Mr. Gwatkin being *"Dixie Professor of Ecclesiastical History, Cambridge."*

He did not miss art-modeling, his only steady job for the last nine years. He had been working at Elwin Porter's Commercial & Fine Arts Studios when he was asked for the first time to pose for a crucifixion. "Why me?" he had asked. "Because of your hungry Arab look," Elwin Porter said. "Grow a beard." They offered him a raise of two dollars an hour. So for the last six years he had hung from crosses constructed from studio easels and six-foot lengths of 2 by 4. He worked in three-hour sessions with a five-minute break every twenty-five minutes. He usually worked six hours a day.

The first few minutes never hurt much. He could watch them watching him and listen to their wisecracking that sounded as if for some reason they were embarrassed. Then he couldn't hold up his head anymore. There was silence and he could hear the timer ticking away. He tried to hold his breath to rest his back muscles but then the next breath hurt even more. His noisy heartbeat had drowned out the timer. He couldn't tell if it was already twenty minutes or only five. The artists were bent over their easels. He could see the irritating old cigar-chewer's bald spot on the top of his head like a surrender to time and understood him better. The commercial art student who had asked to be allowed to come to this class was crying. Then they all had become a blur and he heard Sibelius' *Valse lyrique* that his mother played on the big Boesendorfer piano that made him dizzy because he was sitting underneath the piano to observe the pedals move and to hear the little "bump" sound they made.

Then the timer was ringing and somebody said: "Rest." Elwin Porter and one of the artists removed the upper part of the cross. "Walk around," they said.

The gravel on the terrace announced the arrival of a car. The little red chain-driven Royal Mail truck, a working museum piece, was delivering the post. After a few minutes the gravel rattled again signaling its departure. He got up and left the cottage. The mail was always deposited in The Croft on the hall table that stood between a coat rack and a thick ceramic receptacle holding umbrellas and walking sticks. Resting on top of the table was a paper knife and a bronze East Indian gong that he expected, any day now, to obnounce with its deep doom-filled voice. Four months ago he had sent his latest short story collection to his mother who was stuck behind the Iron Curtain in Hungary. As a girl, his mother had had an English nanny who taught her to listen to the BBC's world service so that she would not forget the language. She had followed that advice all her life. Every day for the past four months he had imagined her reading his stories sitting in her *fauteuil* that was the color of their dead Weimaraner, Ricky. It was the only piece of her furniture that had survived World War II and the 1956 Revolution.

Today there was only one letter, the long-awaited one, an oblong, blue envelope with the legend: *Legiposta* and underneath it: *Air Mail.* He looked at the strangely beautiful gothic handwriting that had become the essence of his mother. They had not seen each other for fifteen years. If he went back to visit he would end up in a concentration camp though now in 1960, the Communist regime cynically allowed some of its citizens to leave the country when they reached the age of sixty-five. His mother had turned sixty-five in January.

He carefully slit open the letter and unfolded it.

My sweet Son,

I had to turn in my passport to receive an exit visa from the Hungarian government before applying for a visa from the British embassy. Hungarian passports now are valid only for three months. The passport office waited until my passport had become invalid before sending it back to me accompanied by your short story collection. It was the first time I had seen your lovely book with your photo on it. Your stories are a great comfort for me. I recognized some of the places you described and my straw Tyrolean hat.

I so wanted to meet your lovely, angelic wife Meg and my beautiful grandchildren, Sibet and Johnyka and your kind and loving in-laws. Beloved, I do not expect that we will see each other again in this life. There does not seem to be the

possibility that the Soviets will ever leave and take their
Hungarian satraps with them. I try not to be bitter. Bitterness
and hate eat into your flesh and that can cause cancer. Even if
you were here you could do nothing to help me. Every week
we hear stories about people killed at the border trying to
escape.
My blessings on all of you,
your loving
Mother.

Moaning like a wounded beast he lifted the padded hammer and struck the gong just as his father-in-law came in to check on the post.

"It's a rather glorious sound, isn't it," his father-in law said.

* * * * * *

Walking back to the stable the gravel began to sound like his footsteps in the deep snow during the endless retreat from the Dnieper in 1943. When he opened the green cottage door it grated and creaked like something in the nineteen-thirties mystery theater plays he had heard on Radio Budapest. The small room downstairs felt overheated and smelled nauseatingly of bacon. He had not washed up the breakfast dishes nor had he taken upstairs the pajamas that the children had strewn all over the bamboo settee and matching bookcase. His portable typewriter was on the table. He had written a paragraph earlier but now couldn't even force himself to re-read it. His mother's blue airmail letter had become the stimulus for an associative pattern that brought back the full-blown memory of the end of World War II, when he believed for a short time that through writing poetry he could reclaim his humanity that had been so

49

thoroughly waylaid in the last four years, only to find that his poems had less value—even to himself— than a head of cabbage. On the bookcase next to the ancient Phillips radio was a packet of black and white photos of his mother that in the evenings he used as flash cards so that Meg and the children would not meet a stranger. There was one of her in a black lace off-shoulder dress looking pensive as if, having glimpsed the future, she was holding back tears. She was incredibly beautiful like a night-blooming cereus concentrating all her loveliness for that moment in time. There were other less dramatic photos of her: picking wild flowers in a field; standing next to her Nonius mare, her riding skirt draped over her arm; sitting at the piano, her head turned toward the photographer. He had taken that picture himself with his first box camera. He shoved the photos away realizing he had been looking at his mother as if she were already dead. To distract himself he turned on the wireless. The BBC program already in progress was about a condemned man in California, a mass murderer tagged the "Lovers' Lane Killer," who after nine years on death row was soon to be executed. He switched off the wireless but his thoughts stayed with the man about to die. He too, had once awaited execution, standing against a weather-beaten green carriage gate. He was afraid of the pain that the bullets would cause but the real horror came from the thought of being alone, trapped in a black, seamless, suffocating, timeless nothing. They were shouting questions at him from behind their guns. He had no answers to give. After a while they lowered their rifles and led him away.

He sat down at the table again and looked over at the sink and the towel rack hung with a souvenir dishtowel from the Lake District depicting Beatrix Potter's Peter Rabbit.

"That's really the Easter Bunny," Johnny had said. Tonight the children would be dyeing eggs ready for Easter Sunday. He hoped the weather would be fine for the egg hunt. Then without any transition the reality of Good Friday came upon him, of Jesus, his tortured body bent over carrying the upper beam of the heavy cross on his way to Calvary. He would be nailed on with real nails. No timer would ring and nobody would shout: "Rest." He beheld the suffering, pain-wracked Man trudging toward Golgotha. He began to cry.

* * * * * *

On Sunday morning he awoke early. Above his head the skylight set into the sloping roof had become an abstract painting, a pale-green color field dominating the branches of the cherry tree. His watch on the floor beside him said: 5:30. Meg and the children were sleeping. Downstairs he pulled on his jeans, sweatshirt, socks and boots. He stoked up the fire, careful not make any noise and went outside promising himself once more to put graphite on the door hinges. The intermittent March wind touched the tree branches and the primroses on the banks around The Croft. He walked toward the outside WC, staying on the grass at the edge of the terrace to avoid the noisy gravel. He could see down into the dell where clumps of wood violets and daffodils formed small congregations. He faintly heard the invisible sheep on the shrouded hills around him. The shingle on the beach rolled lazily commanded by a slow, rhythmic clapping of the sea.

After he flushed the toilet and stepped outside to go back to bed he had to shield his eyes from the unbearable majesty of the rising sun. The door of the WC faced east. Turning right he was surrounded by a clear white light that rendered the cottage thirty yards away invisible. There was total silence as if the earth, having received the knowledge of the Lord told the March wind to stop blowing and the sea to desist. He fell to his knees. Seeing the vision of the unveiled Face he lay down covering his head with his arms expecting the black, seamless, suffocating nothing that had waited for him since he had been led away from the green, peeling carriage gate, but instead there was light without any shadows. He closed his eyes overwhelmed by love.

A Fable

It was five in the morning, the time when, in his experience, the condemned was awakened to be led out. At five in the morning his stomach, independently from his thoughts, remembered another time, another country, though consciously he was only thinking of a lone goldfish he had put in one of the horses' drinking troughs. His grandson had won it with a well-placed tennis ball at the Alachua County Fair. There was no way he could tell the boy at the age of five that they should not bring the fish home in its cramped plastic jail that had made his own body want to stretch to burst asunder the walls of punishment cells that like some indelible tattoo were stamped onto his brain. There was no way he could explain that he only wanted to spare him the pain of seeing his goldfish floating belly-up in a glass bowl. Since the fish had been named there was nothing else he could do but bring it home. Trying somehow to shield the boy from pain, he recollected reading in an Extension publication about the maintenance of cattle and horse troughs and proposed one of their horses' troughs as a home for Goldy.

At the next morning's feeding he had expected to see a dead fish floating on the surface of the water trough, but other than bits of grass and a single white egret feather there was nothing.

A month later when he was skimming the water with a bucket he had seen Goldy in the depths of the murky trough.

"What time is it?" his wife asked.

"A few minutes past five."

"Did you look at the outside temperature?"

"It was just one tick above freezing."

"Do you think the lettuce will survive?"

"I don't see why not. They had time to get hardened. They went in way before the potatoes. Go back to sleep."

"You too," she said and patted his hand. But he couldn't sleep. He got up and padded out to the kitchen. The garden planting diary lived on the top of the bar in the corner next to two Bibles (a Thompson's annotated reference bible with a King James Version text and an ultrathin reference edition of the 1973 New International Version), a book of daily readings, *Highways of the Spirit*, a 1924 London publication of the Student Christian Movement that he had inherited from his father-in-law, and a leather dice-cup holding chopsticks. Every morning he sat on one of the bar stools and read the lessons for the day. He had less discipline with the psalms. He read them according to his need. Lately he often read the third psalm: "There are many who say of me: 'There is no help for him in God.' But thou, O Lord art my shield, my glory, the one who lifts up my head."

The garden diary said that they had planted the lettuce seeds on November 12. The potatoes were planted on Valentine's Day as usual. When they first came to Florida in 1951 with their four-week-old baby girl, a neighboring farmer, Mr. Parker, told them that in North Florida sensible people planted their Irish potatoes on Valentine's Day. Unless they got a hard freeze they were safe.

He couldn't get Goldy out of his mind. Goldy alone in the murky water. Goldy an inadvertent symbol for the Remnant. He lived among western Christians, many of whose theologians, bishops, priests, and ministers preached Christianity based on human sagacity that had made it easily fit in with the culture religion of *equitas* that enshrined *Tolerance* but abhorred God's triune manifestation, its revelation in the resurrected Son. In the same way that King Nebuchadnezzar's chief eunuch had renamed Daniel, they wanted to rename the One beyond their ken to name.

He felt sadness pressing down on him as if he were lying under a fallen beam in a bomb-damaged house. The pain he felt was overwhelming. He listened to it, trying to sort it out as he had tried in the war to sort out the sounds around him, believing that if he had classified them correctly he was safe provided it wasn't heavy artillery, mortars, or B-25 bombers. He could not classify this pain. There was no demarcation between the physical and the mental, no green line that would indicate one side or the other.

He dressed and went outside. The dogs came out of their kennel to dance around him sounding their happy cry to greet him but went back to their houses. They knew that it was too early for breakfast. He unchained the pasture gate. The chain touching the gate gave a short musical note. The lower-lying pasture was glittering white in the early morning darkness. The horses were outside the barn facing east toward the woods like worshipers standing in the nave of an Orthodox cathedral. Frodo and Fancy, the two white ponies, looking heraldic, trotted up to join them. With pricked ears they watched a small band of grazing deer.

The deer had jumped over the fence from the San Felasco nature preserve. In the total silence he could hear them crop the winter grass, then one of the horses stomped the ground and the deer froze into statues of speed and grace. They were all waiting, watching the white light expand as if seeing the moment of creation bringing forth a streak of green that no color chart had ever captured, then light pink deepening into rich purple, a royal robe edged with gold flung over it.

Birds began to sing, the deer were released, and in his joy he rehearsed with the psalmist: "Blessed is the man whom thou choosest, O Lord, and causest to approach thee."

Pain that seemed to have made a constant abode in him for the past few years had disappeared with the peculiar effect of a struck guitar string that would not resonate. He remembered the pain but its sting had gone as if to teach him that though there were no endings there were always beginnings that could come in the blinking of an eye, a trumpet blast, or with the daily aesthetic glory of a sunrise.

The sky was blue now with clouds flung like gossamer scarves in an arc against it. Samba, the lightning-struck chestnut thoroughbred, who against all odds reached Olympic levels in dressage, came up to nudge him in the back. It was feeding time.

After all the horses and ponies were fed, he went around to inspect the water troughs. Goldy's, the largest one, was right by the barn. He checked the hose connections, and the automatic water level device. Sometimes the horses knocked it off or chewed on the hoses. The mineral block on its pedestal next to the trough would last another week. He bent over the water to check on Goldy. The murky water reminded him of the Danube of his boyhood with its greenish color. The Danube was not blue no matter how many times his mother played the *Blue Danube Waltz* on the Bösendorfer in the music room. There were bits of grass

56

floating on the surface of the water. Underneath, like reddish-gold jeweled Christian symbols, fishes were swimming slowly in procession.

He lived in a world where everyone did that which was right in his own eyes and there was no open vision. There were eight fish, a large one and seven smaller ones, in the trough. He knew that Carol Law, their generous neighbor two miles down the road bred fish, tropical birds, and plants for landscapes, but he also knew that it didn't really matter how the fish came to be there. Walking back to the house he prayed for humility to learn to give up his intellectual self-image, accept the revelation, and be thankful.

Kate, Kate

The trees, the color of offset ink no. 3-5310, "Spring Green," curved around the lake as if seen through a fish-eye lens. The lake pulsed with silver flashes, a giant firefly trying to attract its mate. He was watching Kalinowsky, waist-deep in the lake, unreeling a trapline. A cracked, black-male voice was singing, "Alleluiah, band of glory." "Alleluiah," he sang with him, seeing the screen door with the tear where Kalinowsky's 30/30 bullet passed through at the height where the baby's head would have been but for some reason wasn't.

"Andre!" Kalinowsky called from under the water that kept on flashing over his face, arranging and rearranging his straight blond hair in slow motion, synchronized with the silver flashes. The voice was singing, "Alleluiah, revive us again," and he was swimming toward shore pulling Kalinowsky with him, the pain in his lungs unbearable. He knew that they both would die but

59

he couldn't let go because it would be easier to die than to have Meg and Lee see Kalinowsky's bloated body on the shore. Meg always brought Lee down for her afternoon swim. The telephone woke him. It was his son-in-law. "Andre," he said, "you're a grandfather. Her name is Katherine Ilona. Seven pounds, fifteen ounces and twenty-one inches long. We'll call her Kate."

"Thank God. How is Lee?"

"She's fine. Meg'll tell you. She's on her way home."

"Is the baby all right?" Something didn't sound right.

"She isn't very active yet. . . . I'd better get some sleep now. I've been up since Tuesday morning."

He looked at the clock radio. One-fifteen. Through the screen door he heard the trees moving in the breeze. Fireflies were signaling each other at the edge of the woods. There was a terrible, familiar fear in his stomach which he tried to explain away by remembering that it was always early in the morning when he was awakened to be led or wheeled out to face something threatening. He heard his son-in-law say in his doctor's voice: "She isn't very active." She hadn't been very active for two days before she was born.

"Please, Lord."

Hearing his voice, the dog sleeping outside the screen door on the wooden deck thumped his tail.

Meg arrived home at two o'clock. She had been substitute "labor coach."

"I was the first to see her emerge," she said. "She looks a lot like Lee; the shape of her head, the hair line, lots of hair." She got into bed beside him.

"Jeremy said she wasn't very active." He wanted to hear something reassuring.

"Jeremy was so sweet. We are lucky with our children's spouses."

"I want to know about the baby." He wanted to be told that everything was all right.

"They didn't bring her back after the suctioning. That isn't a very good sign."

"What are you saying?"

"I don't know. Maybe it's nothing. I'm a psychologist, not an MD. I wish I could tell you more."

He couldn't go to sleep wondering why Meg didn't say anything about their becoming grandparents. They used to talk about it before Kate was born. Was it because Kate wouldn't live? Kate, Kate. He was willing the baby to keep going. In '44 on the Eastern Front he got very drunk. Alcoholic poisoning drunk. His comrades had saved him by talking him into going on when all he wanted to do was lie down in the snow. It had been twenty-five below. He remembered that his appointment with Dr. Baker was for today. He had lived in Florida most of his adult life. Skin cancer was a real possibility.

* * * * * *

The editorial department of the Institute of Agricultural Research was a part of the university and was housed in the Thurston W. Culpepper Hall, one of the original brick structures from the 1800s. His office, a high-ceilinged room with a window, looked down on a courtyard between two "instructional" buildings. The window was a new double-glazed one that was supposed to seal out heat, cold, and sound. It coped with the elements but not with the students. During class changes the shuffling of feet and the high-pitched laughter reminded him of the Devon coastline, the sound of shingle shifted on the beaches by the incoming tide and the shrill cries of sea gulls. He had been irritated all week by the choice of the cover color for a series of

61

bulletins on equine illnesses. He wondered who had chosen green for texts on infectious anemia and sleeping sickness.

The phone buzzed. He was wanted on line three.

"Daddy." It was Lee reporting that she was home, discharged from the hospital. She and Jeremy were on their way to visit Kate.

"How is she?" "Daddy, she's in the intensive care unit on a hundred percent oxygen."

"Oh, Lord, please."

"You should come and see her, Daddy. It isn't what you think. She looks very sweet even with the tubes."

* * * * * *

He looked down at the courtyard. It was empty—classes were in session. The Coca Cola man was filling up his machine. It sounded like a very long machine-gun burst. The phone buzzed. He stiffened as if he had expected someone to shoot at him from below. One of the buttons on the phone kept blinking as it buzzed, then another and another. All the buttons blinked, then the red "hold" light came on signaling that there was a message for him in the main office.

He went out to the corridor that with its smells and peeling paint reminded him of his school in Hungary. Only the plaster busts of long-dead philosophers were missing. Most of his schoolmates were long dead too—dead of gunshot wounds, starvation, bomb fragments, hangings.

The message was in his slot in the carrousel. A piece of paper 5 and 1/2 x 2 and 1/2. Very simple; a place for the date, the message, the time of the call. He was afraid to look at it. It could destroy his life as effectively as a land mine could. He looked at the message. "Please call Ellie Hollister."

62

"Ellie!" He was shouting with relief. It wasn't a call from the hospital.

"She's in University Hospital, in intensive care."

"Have you seen her?"

"No. Not yet. I think I might be catching a cold."

"You ought to go and see her as soon as you can."

"Please pray for us."

"I am praying. We all are. People are phoning the church office all the time wanting to know about Kate."

* * * * * *

At ten-thirty Edna came into his office to empty the trashcan. The floors had been swept earlier. The janitorial staff started work at five.

"How's Kate?"

"She's on a respirator now."

"I already told Calvin that she was taken into intensive care. Calvin goes to Mount Moriah. They are strong pray-ers." From her overall pocket she gave him a cassette tape. He put it in the tape player.

"It's homemade," Edna said. A cracked, black-male voice was singing: "Alleluia, band of glory, revive us again."

"Do you like it?" She was watching his face.

"I heard it in a dream." He didn't know if it was the beginning or the middle of the song. "Can you believe . . . in a dream?"

"Yes," Edna said matter-of-factly.

* * * * * *

It was half past four. He was parked in the Veteran's Hospital circular drive waiting for Meg, watching the door for the first

63

glimpse of her face before she collected herself for the outside world. That first glimpse always told him if one of her patients had succeeded in suicide or if a patient who seemed capable of coping had returned to the hospital again, overwhelmed by the impatience of the world, disoriented by its hucksterism that sold soft drinks, politicians, religion, and cars with the same technique of false sincerity and ballyhoo.

Meg came outside, stopped beside a man in a wheelchair, then hurried on to the car and got in.

"Put on your seat belt." He had read nothing in her face.

"What did Dr. Baker have to say?" Absentmindedly, she fastened her seat belt.

"I'm OK. He told me to wear a hat when I'm in the sun." He concentrated on the traffic. Archer Road had six lanes where University of Florida students raced their daily grand prix. Once past McDonald's, driving needed less concentration. He turned onto one of the interstate entrances, and drove on I-75 for two exits. With the out-of-state license plates passing them he usually pretended they too were on holiday and would soon be stopping at a beautiful place.

"Did you phone the children?" she asked.

"I was afraid of waking them. They are exhausted."

"There wouldn't have been anything to report," she said.

"Have you talked with your M.D. friends?"

"Yes," she mumbled, looking straight ahead.

"I can't hear you over the air conditioner."

"The babies who survive for three days usually make it."

Kate, Kate, he thought. Kate, Kate.

"I would like to close my eyes for a few moments," Meg said. "I am not rejecting your company."

* * * * * *

64

They were driving by a rookery. Cattle egrets were flying in, serene white birds sailing over I-75, over cars and huge diesel trucks to land clumsily on trees already crowded with birds like untidily dropped laundry bundles marked with orange slashes. Then they were off I-75. At the stop sign before they turned onto the county road, Meg woke up.

"I didn't think phlox would still be around in April," she said.

The road dipped then climbed again past a hilly pasture dotted with miniature horses giving the impression of a hobbit encampment. At the other side of the road a large plastic sign in front of a white frame church declared: "FEMALE PROTECTIVE SOCIETY." He had never seen anybody entering or leaving the church but the lawn around it was neatly cut.

He turned onto County Road 241, which could have been the Devon road leading to Exeter, to the cathedral and the Ship Inn just off cathedral close. It was the pub where he drank ale on his day off just as Sir Francis Drake drank his a few centuries earlier. The other thing they had in common was St. Augustine, Florida. Sir Francis had bombarded it from the sea but had never visited the town. He, on the other hand, drove to St. Augustine whenever he could to look at Fort San Marcos, the coquina walls rising majestic and undefeated. He loved the creaking of carriage wheels over cobblestones and the sound of horses' hooves striking the pavement. He loved to walk the narrow streets with their balconied Spanish houses, then rest in Trinity church where light came filtered through stained-glass windows that kept the altar and furnishings in peaceful Victorian gloom smelling of furniture polish, candle wax, old incense, musty prayer books, and a perpetual Ash Wednesday reminder of dusty kneelers.

He hadn't always felt this way about St. Augustine. When he first came to the U.S. he wanted to leave all things European behind, the complications and restrictions as well as the architecture. Even in England, mother of parliaments, he had to report to the police whenever he changed digs, and it was the Ministry of Labour who decided whether he would work in a coal mine, cotton mill, gas works, or a mental hospital kitchen. In the U.S. he was only required to register once a year at any post office. That was all. He could choose his own work and when he became a citizen, his vote could elect a President of the United States. He wanted to be a real American, a simple man of the soil, a Florida cracker with forty acres and a mule. He got the forty acres—rented land. Instead of the mule he had an old, grey Fordson utility tractor. He worked on Mr. Durance's ranch, where he rounded up scrub and crossbred cows on 32,000 acres of scrubland. He was hot and tired most of the time, his jeans black and slimy from the horse's sweat. Being a ranch hand wasn't at all what he had seen in the cinemas. There was no singing. In real life when he wasn't chasing cows or loading them into trucks, he was carrying sacks from the feed mill.

County Road 241 crossed over I-75. The power lines running parallel with the interstate highway were filled with egrets reminding him of the glass birds clipped to the Christmas tree branches in his boyhood. He turned off 241 and drove through a low brick entranceway onto a private road that divided to flow around a huge oak. He was looking at the green earth, a curving, rounded shape that at the same time was restful and exciting, that made him want to shout halleluiah not as a response to a liturgical command but as a shout of thankfulness, a lifting of hands, and he saw trees transformed into uplifted arms and he heard the singing that was not always audible to people deafened by the sound of their own creations.

He stopped at their mailbox.

"Anything?"

"Just bills and junk mail," Meg said. In his cowboy period when Lee was 17 months old and they were renting a two-room shack, even junk mail had seemed miraculous. Prisoners, especially political prisoners, don't receive fliers inviting them to executive seminars, and nobody tries to sell them life insurance or cemetery plots. Those ads had reaffirmed his humanity that had been reduced to a serial number. He read the ads after the evening milking, sitting on the front steps because it was cooler there than in the house. The house—wood siding, tin roof, no insulation—consisted of two small rooms, a kitchen, and a screened porch that had become Lee's nursery. Every day she sat by the screen door, talking to her cats on the outside. The porch had a sink and a hand pump. Most mornings when he primed the pump a frog would jump out of it, land on the sink, then wait for him to leave. The frog was named Prince. Lee talked to Prince just like she talked to her cats. There were mornings when he awoke to Lee's baby chatter and knew that he had been given everything: life, love, and the ability to love. And he had the forty acres of rented land that nobody could just walk in and take away.

Half a mile from the house was Turtle Lake. He was standing on the sand of the lakeshore when he first saw Kalinowsky. He had gone to set out the traplines—they had found that even garfish were edible if the skin was removed before cooking—and noticed a strange green car driving slowly down the road. It was an old Pontiac with an Indianhead hood ornament. The car stopped opposite him and a man got out. He was tall, with narrow shoulders that made him seem even taller. He had a greasy army fatigue cap on his straight, blonde hair and was wearing a long-sleeved flannel shirt even in the ninety-eight-degree heat.

"You own the land here?"

"Renting. I am renting." Questions made him panicky. He was ready to show the palms of his hands, the calluses that were big enough now to keep him out of labor camps where class enemies were sent. He was sinking into memories that made his heart beat so loud that it was almost impossible for him to hear anything else.

"That's what I'm looking for."

"What?"

"Land to rent . . . I . . . am . . . looking . . . for . . . land . . . to . . . rent . . . Understand?"

* * * * * *

The woods began a few yards past their mailbox. The dogs, recognizing the sound of the car, began to streak across the first paddock next to their son's house. By the time he turned the car onto the driveway beside the vegetable garden, the dogs were there, showing with their clamor what good and faithful dogs they were, defending their home all day long.

"You hairy phonies," he said, getting out of the car. "I saw you at Anne and John's playing with Clarence." Clarence, his son's dog whose well-mixed antecedents had produced what amounted to a new large breed, was licking his hand. Tallulah, an ancient vizsla, was licking his other hand. Ralphie, who was part dachshund, part basset, tugged at his ankle. Then suddenly they left him and began to bark in earnest. A panel truck with "Curtis Newsome Well Drilling and Pumps" sign on its side was turning into their drive.

"He's come to check the pump," Meg said. "You go in and open the windows."

A gravel path divided around a big hickory tree and what looked like a hut circle that he had built three years ago in memory of the prehistoric sites he had seen on Dartmoor in England. Now the rocks were moss-covered as if they had sprung from the ground right here to surround the velvety petunias guarded by tall irises with drawn swords. The house, its rough-cut cedar siding blending with the woods, had become a part of nature. When he opened the front door he could look straight through the sliding glass door that opened onto a cracker back porch with dogwoods behind it. Just two weeks ago the dogwoods had looked like snow-covered trees; now they were transformed by their lacy green leaves into thin, long-legged art deco creatures.

He pushed back the sliding door. Behind it the screen was torn a few feet up from the ground. Panic started in the middle of his chest, the pendulum of the grandfather clock banging away, the reverberations making him deaf. He was trying to remember two days ago when he had noticed Ralphie inside the house though no doors had been left open. Ralphie must have busted through the screen door but unreasoning fear cancelled logic and the movie began to roll, the pictures held for a moment, then moved on fast enough to blur the edges. Then sound was added, the sound of a 30/30 going off in a small house.

Kalinowsky was holding his rifle that he didn't believe in unloading, pointing it straight at the screen door. He was watching Kalinowsky because he couldn't make himself turn around and look at his baby daughter. He reached for the sharp boning knife Meg had given him to carry because they couldn't afford a snake-bite kit. He reached for his knife but didn't use it. He turned and looked at the torn screen then began to run to the kitchen. Lee was there, sitting under the table, her little hands covering her ears.

Two weeks later he had saved Kalinowsky from drowning, not because he liked Kalinowsky or because it was the right, natural thing to do but because it was more important to him, more important than his own life, that his family wouldn't see a dead, bloated body lying on the white, sandy shore of Turtle Lake. He opened the windows. So many times he had thought he had found paradise—this house was the latest. He had always wanted ceramic tile floors, a floor-to-ceiling bookcase with a ladder, a good, working fire-place, and a high ceiling. He had them all, even the forty acres, yet his granddaughter was in the ICU because she couldn't breathe on her own. People did not die in paradise.

Meg came in.

"Mr. Newsome said the casing is cracked. But we're still under warranty, and he'll get us a new pump."

"He really is a decent man."

"I told him about Kate," Meg said. "His mother is part of the First Baptist prayer chain. He already called her from the truck."

* * * * * *

A new wing was being added to the University Hospital. The temporary walls, set inside the shell, resembled a cattle chute through which people shuffled as if on the last stage of a long drive. The ground floor of the finished section was a huge room with large sofas placed in "conversation groups"— a giant family's living room. Sitting on the sofas were out-of-scale people who looked like airline passengers with missed connections: bored and at the same time tense, waiting for the call that would allow them to go on with their lives.

He watched Meg walk to the security desk and use one of their phones. Nobody ever felt the need to challenge Meg. She came back with a plastic visitor's pass.

"Clip it to your shirt pocket," she said. Hers was already clipped to her dress. They were the only people getting off the elevator on the third floor. An arrow pointed toward the intensive care unit. They went through a double swinging door

"I phoned Jeremy from the security desk," Meg said. "If you stand by the window with the Venetian blind, you'll be able to see Kate. Her bed is right under it." She kissed him, turned, and went inside.

He stood by the window. Light seeped through the blind, then with a sudden movement the blind rose and he saw Jeremy's smiling face and beyond him green-clad people in constant motion as if in a pantomime, moving among glass boxes occupied by wired baby dolls. Fastened to the walls were other electronic boxes that pulsed with the steadiness of waves lapping a seahore. Attached to the stainless-steel bed closest to the window was a piece of cheerful, yellow poster board that said "Kate" in Lee's clear, schoolteacher's handwriting. Lee was standing beside the bed, her face glowing as if with a beatific vision. Kate seemed big compared with the premature babies around her. Her head, turned sideways, showed her round, dimpled cheek and turned-up nose. The breathing tube did not distort her little face.

* * * * * *

The cars in the parking lot gleamed with the reflected overhead lights. There was a gentle April breeze that brought with it the smell of the ocean an hour's drive away.

"What does it really mean that she is on a hundred percent oxygen?" He had gone in after all. It wasn't enough to look at Kate from the window. He had scrubbed and put on a paisley gown. Inside there was the sound of constant beeping as if the machines were talking to each other but the people didn't look

71

like automatons anymore. One of the nurses adjusted Kate's IV. She and Lee smiled at each other as if the two of them shared a happy secret. The nurse looked eight months pregnant.

"I told you, Daddy, Kate is a beautiful little girl," Lee had said. It was then that he had reached out and touched the child, not afraid to know her anymore.

"Hundred percent oxygen means that there is no going higher," Meg said.

The inky sky was dotted with stars that glittered like cheap costume jewelry. He didn't want to live in a world without Kate.

* * * * * *

The dogs barked. He got up from the rocking chair and opened the front door. The salmon colored azaleas were blooming against the background of the grey of the cedar siding. The gravel path was covered with the gold leaves of the hickory tree. The dogwood had red leaves and bright, red berries. It was the strangest Florida November he could remember. The temperature was eighty degrees and his hut circle was filled with not only coleus and purple amaranth of the late summer but paper-whites as well.

The dogs barked again. A car had started off at the other side of the woods. They must have dropped by Anne and John's. The dogs raced across the first paddock but then turned back. The car was turning into their driveway.

* * * * * *

He carried in the molded car seat. Strapped in, Kate looked like a jet pilot after ejection. Meg carried a bag with the diapers and food. Jeremy and Lee had left straightaway. They were late for a concert.

Once inside he put the car seat on the dining room table. Kate's eyes were brimming with tears. "I'll get you out in a minute." Her arms reached out to him.

"In one second you'll be free, Kate, and then your grandmother will feed you."

"I'm warming it now," Meg said from the kitchen. "Why don't you go and sit in your rocker. She'll like that."

He was holding the baby to himself, slowly rocking. They were looking at the woods, the bare, dark trunks of the trees allowing them to see one of the still-green pastures, the gold leaves on the ground making a clear demarcation between the living and the dead. He lifted Kate over his head, overwhelmed with thankfulness and love, and the heavens opened and he watched the prayers of the First Baptist, lights blinking, bells pinging as if somebody had hit the jackpot on a super pinball machine, then fireworks exploded, the prayers of Calvin's church and Edna's shaking the heavens. Underneath it all rose the steady, golden incense of his own church upholding this little girl.

He was holding up Kate, seeing the one tooth in her wide-open mouth, her eyes and mouth laughing in a silent baby laugh.

"You think your grandfather is peculiar, don't you?" They were all peculiar he thought; they believed that they had a common Father who loved them equally, that though their bodies would be destroyed they would see God, and they prayed for one another that they might be healed. Yet all this time searching for paradise, he had not realized that he was already part of the kingdom; he had not recognized his fellow-citizens all around him.

"How about Kate coming to Grandmother." Meg was reaching for her. "We are going to the kitchen to find something for Kate to eat."

Kate was phuffing, her latest experiment in sound. She looked back at him over Meg's shoulder, laughing.

All Loves Excelling
Eucharist in Rite One

Having rais' d me to look up,
In a cup
Sweetly he doth meet my taste.
But still being low and short,
Farre from court,
Wine becomes a wing at last.

But with it alone I flie
To the skie
Where I wipe mine eyes, and see
What I seek, for what I sue;
Him I view,
Who hath done so much for me.

—George Herbert (d. 1633)

The choir processed from the entrance singing: "Love Divine, All Loves Excelling." Saint Peter's Victorian interior smelled incongruously English here in the Diocese of Florida. The crucifer processed by him and he could already single out Jessica's voice in the choir, a sweet

English soprano that had hardly changed since he first heard it in St. Margaret's, Todmorden, Lancashire, a few years after the end of World War II. He had escaped the communists in Hungary and had made his way to the U.S. zone in Salzbtug, Austria, where he had signed up as a European Voluntary Worker to be shipped to the United Kingdom. He had mistaken St. Margaret's with its carved, dusty reredos, massive, oak pulpit, and brass eagle adorning the lectern for a Roman Catholic church until a woman shared her prayer book with him,' and he realized that what he had taken for mangled Latin was in fact English. Later he had learned by heart the beautiful Elizabethan cadences of Cranmer's translation, but most of all it was Jessica's voice in the choir that had made him into an Anglican.

He remained one during what he later called his first exile, when the Ministry of Labour sent him to Ebbw Vale in Wales to be a coal miner. A small cave-in had trapped him underground for twenty hours and had induced claustrophobia that made stepping into the cage to descend to the depths of the mine five and a half days a week pure hell. It took all the limited energy he derived from tea, unsweetened porridge served without milk, and fish and chips twice a week to keep himself from screaming.

He earned four pounds sterling a week, one pound more than he had made in the cotton mill, and he was able to save a small amount each month. He was saving for their house. He wanted to show Jessica's father, a fishmonger and fruiterer with a shop on Styan Street, that he was worthy to be considered a future son-in-law. In Lancashire there seemed to be an unwritten law stating that a couple could not marry unless they had a house. He didn't realize that "having" a house didn't necessarily mean owning one, but then he didn't know anything about buying houses either since in his own family nobody had ever bought one. They had inherited the land and the buildings—even a house in Vienna and

76

a villa in Italy—paintings, silver, smelly old Turkish carpets, furniture, and family portraits.

In Ebbw Vale, Jessica's letters kept him going. He had read them over and over again. He loved even the sight of them, the letters becoming a real presence in his life, turning him into an idolater. He still remembered her last letter:

. . . . You and God are the only constants in my life, and God is too far above me and too distant. You're far above me too—in all ways. Please keep on loving me—forever if possible. I shall always love you.

When she wrote that letter she was already going out with the American she was to marry.

* * * * * *

His first exile ended years later when they met at Saint Savior's. It was after Mass. She was standing beside the coffee urn that had been brought outside from the parish hall to take advantage of the cool, 69°F, Florida winter Sunday. She was wearing a high-necked, white blouse with a navy blue shawl draped around her shoulders, a navy blue skirt that almost reached her ankles, and low- heeled open shoes. He remembered that she always hated closed shoes even in the cold English winters. Her eyes were the same young eyes that made it seem as if they had never been apart, as if the history of the intervening years was only fiction created by an over-inventive writer hell-bent on complicating his plot.

"Your hair is gray," she said. She still spoke with an indefinable English accent. Her hair was tied back. She had worn it the same way in Todmorden. He was thinking of her last letter that he had recited all these years: "Please keep on loving me--forever if possible." He had. God help him, he had.

"Did you know that I would be here?"

"Yes," she had said.

She had gone through an "amicable" divorce six months ago. Her children were grown. She had danced for a few years in the corps de ballet of a small ballet company. Her children and ballet had kept her marriage going. Most of the time she had known where he was. She had even seen him six years ago in Coral Gables. On a bus. Something like a scene from Dr. Zhivago. It had made her cry for a week.

"You haven't changed," he said.

"You either."

But he had. He was married. He had children and grandchildren. He was family-owned.

"I still have your last letter," he said.

That was their second beginning.

* * * * * *

"'Let not your hearts be troubled, neither let them be afraid.'" The pulpit was elevated, giving the impression that Fr. Langlais, St. Peter's rector, was standing on the prow of a sailing ship to see better the obstacles in its path.

"The Lord was preparing his disciples for his imminent death on the cross. He was saying goodbye, knowing that their hearts were troubled, knowing that human love always carried with it the dreadful certainty, the built-in risk of losing the beloved."

Father Langlais was looking at him. On Friday when Jessica had told him that she couldn't go on the way they were, the shock was identical to the one he had received on hearing of his father's death, and the fear was the same fear he had felt in Budapest in 1945 when—awaiting his own turn—he had watched his fellow prisoners swing from ropes attached to the horizontal

78

bar of the goal post on a soccer field. But this time everything had been turned upside down because now instead of fearing the pain of death he feared the pain of life. He might have to go on living for years knowing that Jessica didn't love him anymore.

He tried to remember the times she did love him to blot out a reality that was like a frozen lake inside him. Longfellow counseled inward stillness to bring inner healing, but this wasn't inward stillness. He had become a voodoo zombie who walked, talked, smiled, made civilized conversation, and drove on roads hedged with grass and flowers, which seemed to wilt whenever he looked at them. He had become a comic book character in a land of drought and darkness, a land where no one traveled and no one lived, where pain bloomed like yellow poison flowers. He should have confessed to God, but he could never confess Jessica a misdoing, because that would have meant deliberately forgetting, erasing the picture of the first time he had seen her in Lancashire and had felt as if swallows were swooping around him touching his face with soft wingtips. For no reason at all, that had made him cry. She was sixteen at the time.

Jessica was looking down at him from the front row of the choir loft, though he wasn't sure if she really saw him without her glasses. She believed that wearing glasses impeded her singing. She also believed that one had to run the tap water for a minute before filling up the teakettle. He loved her idiosyncrasies that he had never suspected when they had known each other in Todmorden. But back then he had not yet made her into his totem to worship instead of God, defying the commandment about bowing down to other gods, even though he knew beyond the shadow of a doubt that the language of the Scriptures was not merely the result of an historical accident or some antiquated cultural conditioning.

79

"We think we can't endure losing our beloved. Yet we know that eventually one of us must mourn the other. But Jesus did not leave us comfortless. He sent the Comforter to be with us even in our most profound sorrows. We are never alone. Never."

He wanted to stand up and shout: look at me, what about me? He was a dead man in a world transformed into purgatory.

* * * * * *

"'Almighty and most merciful Father, we have erred and strayed from thy ways like lost sheep, we have followed too much the devices and desires of our own hearts, we have offended against thy holy laws. . . . '" The pain that lived equally in his head and in his heart overwhelmed him, and he remembered a line of the general confession in the Church of England's Book of Common Prayer that truly described his own state; "And there is no health in us." He was filled with pain that had reached a point where death had become the only viable nostrum to end his torment. He knew that God did not desire his death but rather that he turn from his wickedness and live. There could be no absolution without repentance. His mouth said the right penitential words, but his heart had become a big, black manta ray that wrapped itself around the pictures of Jessica: Jessica sitting on the park bench, at sixteen already stricken by tragedy because she was too old to become a first-class ballerina, Jessica in her knitted cap looking like a fairy child, Jessica, the woman, the Modigliani nude with the magic eyes. He could not give up his pictures, he could not press them into an album like dried flowers to transform them into emotionless memories. There was no surgery, no laser technique that could separate them without killing him. God surely must know that.

* * * * * *

From this distance, from where he was sitting, nothing seemed to have changed: Jessica's black robe and white cotta looked exactly like the ones she had worn at St. Margaret's, Todmorden; the way she held her music made her into a Hummel figurine that had been etched onto his heart, a heart that remembered from thirty years ago an identical, unbearable pain, a feeling of defenselessness, knowing that he couldn't stop the pain or its cause no matter what. It was as if his sin contained an ingredient that could thaw out and deliver pain at full strength from thirty years ago.

He had come back from Ebbw Vale after not hearing from Jessica for six weeks. In desperation he even phoned the shop on Styan Street, but her father would only say that she wasn't around and for him to stop phoning. At the mine office he was told that he couldn't leave, that if he did he could be deported. He left Ebbw Vale early on Sunday morning, changed trains in London, and arrived in Todmorden at nine. He wanted to go to the eleven o'clock Choral Mass where at least he could see Jessica. Because he had time to kill, he went to the park; he stood by the large oak and looked toward the bench where he had first seen her sitting in the sunshine. But the bench was empty, the sky overcast. It was a typical Lancashire day.

The café on Lord Street across from the market was open. He ordered a pot of tea and buttered toast. "Then ever they had come here it was Jessica who poured, turning the simple act of drinking tea into a ceremony. It almost made him believe that he was a working-class bloke who belonged. But of course he didn't; he could never belong. He was a bloody foreigner. Nothing could change that. Two of Jessica's girlfriends came into the cafe. It was then that he first heard about the young man from Florida whose

81

grandparents had lived on Styan Street and were friends of Jessica's parents. Jessica was engaged to him, the girls said, and her father made jokes about it, telling his customers that at least the Yanks spoke some kind of English. The girls told him that the American had taken Jessica, her sister Norma, and their mother to Blackpool for a holiday and that they had a card from Jess, showing the Pleasure Beach with the Big Dipper.

At first he didn't feel anything, as if he had been anesthetized to spare him the initial pain that already made his heart beat against his rib cage like a captive bird. He stayed in Todmorden waiting to see Jessica, watching the shop because Jessica's family lived above it, but she never came home. There was only her father in his dirty—white apron serving his customers. He had to be back at the mine in five days or he would be deported to Austria, and the Austrians might decide as a political expediency to send him back to Hungary where he could end up in GULAG for twenty years. He slept less and less, and when he did he dreamt about hourglasses and watched the sand pour out and bury him, bringing a black suffocation that only Jessica could dissolve—but he had to find her first. He was afraid to sleep and began to drink gin in large quantities; that made staying awake even more difficult. His head had become an unsupportable weight where all his thoughts pulsated with electrical bursts that reached his heart with burning probes. On Monday morning at five he was in the cage with his shift mates descending to the depths of the mine. It had ceased to matter to him where he was.

* * * * * *

Thirty years later the same burning probes were touching him. Since Friday when Jessica had said that she was leaving him, he had been beseeching heaven for a sign. On Saturday the sign had been given in the form of a checkrein, a checkrein pulled tight to make him really take notice, to collect him, to make him see that only the pain of separation could cauterize his sin.

On Saturday their best horse had been hit by lightning. Samba was a large thoroughbred gelding, a blue-ribbon winner in dressage and jumping who had lived on their farm since he was a colt. At five, the usual feeding time, he decided to wait out the slight drizzle before going down to the barn, but the drizzle had turned into a hailstorm. He was looking out the window at the black sky when lightning hit a transformer up by the road with a deafening explosion and a blinding flash that blotted out everything. He ran outside into the premature darkness, soaked to the skin in a second, his hair matted to his head. He opened the steel pasture gate afraid of the lightning bolts but even so chaining the gate behind him because gates are always chained fast, running on, blinded by the rain, hearing the whinnying of a horse in distress. Then the snare drums of the barn roof took over, and he saw Samba in the pasture as if in a silent horror movie, down like a newborn colt. He knelt next to him, coaxing, talking, until with a heave the horse struggled to his feet, shaking, wild-eyed. He ripped off his shirt to rub the horse in a useless gesture that made his own helplessness even more apparent. "Where was sweet Jesus, his friend and brother? Where was his Savior? He began to bellow like a wounded beast, praying incoherently, asking for miracles that he didn't expect.

* * * * * *

"'The peace of the Lord be always with you.'" Father Langlais was facing them with outstretched arms.

"'And with your spirit,'" the people answered and turned to each other.

"The peace of the Lord," his wife said.

"The peace of the Lord," he said, looking down at her upturned face. She was the most beautiful woman in his life, the one who had released him from indentured service to the Ministry of Labour, who had given back his humanity, who had restored him to life. They had met in a mental hospital in Hartfordshire, eighteen miles from London. He had been sent to Hartfordshire from Wales by the Ministry of Labour because the miners' union had decided that the foreigners' thick accents constituted a hazard to the rest of the Ebbw Vale miners. She was an American with English family connections, an English-trained psychologist in her first job. He was a porter, the lowest of the low in the hierarchy of the hospital staff, a man indentured for seven years, an untouchable who was advised by his betters not to use the canteen but to take his tea breaks in an alcove set aside for porters. The porters' tan coveralls not only protected their clothing but marked them as outcasts.

At the hospital the porters' quarters were attached to the power plant where they worked. This arrangement had the advantage of providing unlimited hot water in the bathroom that most of his fellow porters used only on weekends. He took a bath after work every day, feeling that it transformed him from a slave to a tourist. The hospital grounds were beautifully landscaped. Herbaceous borders and shrubbery surrounded the buildings, most of which were small enough to pass for country villas. There were imposing flower beds planted with tulips in the distinct colors of the spectrum that turned the beds into giant kaleidoscopes. The flowers, trees, and the deep-green English grass combined to give him a measure of peace. The patients, walking in groups or singly, smiled at him, called him matey, and seemed to accept him as a fellow human being. On some days the patients from the backwards, with their mechanical movements, close-cropped hair, and peculiar smell, came out into their enclosures, and they, too, would wave and shout greetings. As far as the staff was concerned he didn't exist, though the hospital's medical director had asked him for help with a Latin text. Then on a Wednesday afternoon, his life had changed because he saw a girl wheeling an old black bike with a basket attached to its handlebar. She was wearing a square-necked, black and white plaid summer dress with wide straps. Her chestnut-colored hair was cut short. It bounced with her steps as if helping to propel her toward him. Her face was beautiful in a well-bred English way, her head in perfect proportion to her fine body. She had an unmistakable look of gentility. He stopped, unable to move, as if rooted to the English soil that heretofore had rejected him.

"Hello," she said, smiling. She walked toward the building that masqueraded as a rustic brick cottage but that housed schizophrenics. Just before entering the building she turned back and waved. He followed her and waited outside for an hour, listening to the moaning that the building couldn't contain.

A week later they met again. Six months after that they were married.

* * * * * *

"O Lamb of God, that takest away the sins of the world, have mercy upon us. O Lamb of God, that takest away the sins of the world, have mercy upon us. O Lamb of God, that takest away the sins of the world, grant us thy peace.'"

The words of the Agnus Dei reverberated in his chest. He didn't know what he really wanted, what he was asking for, other than forgiveness that would bring not only an absence of pain but peace that the liturgy said passeth all understanding. They all were asking for forgiveness, forgiveness that made the world despise them because the world equated their belief with degradation and softness.

The line moved slowly toward the altar. The choir began to sing: "Let All Mortal Flesh Keep Silence." The people knelt at the altar rail to eat the offered messianic supper. He held up his hands like a hungry beggar reaching for the bread. Once more he was lifted up into a mystical union, not with Christ's memory or with his Spirit but with the risen, glorified Christ, a flesh and blood Christ whose ascended life revealed to him his own future that allowed him now to love without counting costs and returns. He reached for the cup. The wine had become a wing at last.

Libera me, Domine, de morte aeterna

*T*he thatched roof of the whitewashed church was made of reed with the foot-thick edge of the overhang resembling tiny organ pipes laid on their sides, and instead of musical notes they emitted drips of water—slowly falling tears. Though it had stopped raining the sky remained dark, the clouds swirling like a roiling river that was about to drown the rooster, "the symbol of the resurrection, on top of the steeple. The white wash turned into rivulets, splashing down on the ground like milk from an overturned bucket. The soaked clay walls, now an unnatural black, imploded and became one with the mud of the road that rose up to his chest and threatened to suffocate him. A male voice was singing "Libera me, Domine, de morte aeterna."

What woke him was the incongruity of hearing *Deliver me, O Lord, from everlasting death* sung in Latin in the Reformed church that had been built in the seventeenth Century by his great grandfather's father's father in the settlement that shared his family's name. The successful re-reformation by Bishop Peter Pazmany that returned most of the neighboring villages and towns to Rome had only hardened the Calvinist resolve to remove and destroy anything even faintly resembling "Catholic" gestures or symbols, among them the use of Latin and the lighting of candles in church. The church was lit first by whale oil then by kerosene before electricity reached the settlement in the late 1930s. The great illumination for the people came from the Bible translated into Hungarian by Karoli Gaspar at a time when Parliamentary debates were still conducted in Latin. He was only a boy when he learned that Reverend Barna, the Reformed dominie who ruled both the church and the settlement in the manner of a latter day Savonarola, was his Hungarian grandfather's illegitimate son. Men who married Catholic girls from the neighboring villages were forced to find life elsewhere. Even Uncle Iozsef, his father's older brother, whose wife to be was not only Catholic but of the wrong class, had to go into exile as far away as America.

It was his own father who introduced religious tolerance into the settlement when he married a French Catholic and threatened the dominie with death if he didn't keep his mouth shut about the perdition of the Pope and the Roman Catholic Church in general. The dominie did keep his mouth shut, thereby saving his half-brother from the sin of fratricide, and a Catholic chapel was built with stark exposed beams and slit windows suitable for a medieval fortress. Also provided was a rectory that looked the same as the sharecroppers' adobe houses with a set aside five acres for the chaplain's use. His mother named the chapel after Saint Theresa and offered no explanation for her choice. The first chaplain was imported from France. His foreignness and prodigious wine drinking made him acceptable to the men. Their wives fought for the privilege of teaching the French priest Hungarian.

He himself had been baptized Andre, Charles, Jozsef, Pierre-Terrail - over the objection of his Hungarian relatives who resented the fact that three of the names were French---by the Reformed minister-uncle who later prepared him for confirmation. Perhaps because he equally loved and dreaded the dominie, it took him years to overcome a sense of guilt for crossing himself like his mother. His sister was baptized by Fr. de Corsell. It was the first baptism ever held at Saint Theresa's and was attended by the French relatives, still on speaking terms between the World Wars with their "barbarian connection."

For the rest of the inhabitants of the settlement, descendants of Cuman steppe nomads, refugees from Asia who had made their last stand here in the thirteenth century and with luck survived Batu Khan's Golden Horde, nothing much had changed. Then in 1945 the Red Army, the next invaders from the steppes, had turned the settlement into a collective farm and had sent him to a jail. He escaped to England at the age of twenty four, where he met and married Meg. They reached the United States in 1950. Not having any official papers he was admitted on his wife's passport. She was half English, half South Carolinian, the possessor of both a British and a U.S. passport.

* * * * * *

Almost fifty years later he still had nightmares when his wife was away but he had never before dreamt about his whitewashed, thatch-roofed, Hungarian church. The reason for this dream was quite obvious. After the wrench of leaving St. Mark's, their Florida church home for thirty years, to start St. Charles, a traditional parish to be a part of the Continuing Church movement, their consolation for using side tables for altars in members' homes was their conviction that they were the trees of righteousness who had kept the ways of the Lord, knowing that they would receive beauty for ashes, the oil of joy for mourning, and the garment of praise for the spirit of heaviness. When they had reached the point where the house churches were not big enough to hold St. Charles' congregation, they rented a Shriners Clubhouse for their worship. Nine years later they had accumulated altar furnishings, Communion vessels, prayer books, hymnals, candlesticks, a rectory to house their priest and enough money in the building fund to look for land to build on. At that point, their most recent, young rector newcomer to their denomination— his father called vestments KKK robes—decided to design a church service that would "pack them in," that had only the faintest resemblance to an Anglican worship. The people who had built St. Charles' and wished to continue the historic worship had two choices offered them: either accept the services as they were conducted now or leave.

He knew that the nightmare was not caused by their ambitious, immature rector who had only followed the path of wordy success as it was replayed daily on TV. What devastated him was the feeling that God had deserted him, deserted those who had already suffered for their faith having left behind beautiful churches with stained glass windows, organs, choirs and what was the hardest to be separated from, the place from which he expected to be buried, where he had seen his children baptized, confirmed, and married, the place where he would look up and behold a white horse, the Son riding forth in victory. Now there was only claustrophobic silence, where he was mired in mud that clogged up this nose and mouth.

90

His usual nightmares started with the odor of a particular jail. Just as nursing homes have their distinct and overwhelming smells so did the Hungarian military jail where first the Nazis, then the Communists keep their political prisoners. It was an amalgam of urine, sweat permeated by the ever-present fear, the sour breath of starving humans, scorched soup, and the overall harsh scent of disinfectants. The third night of Meg's absence brought on the screams of the tortured and the sobbing and insane babbling of the men in their cells. He, himself, would be standing at attention waiting to be told to sit down on the stone floor, pull up his knees to his chest, and put his arms around them to be hog-tied so that the broom-handle could be inserted between his roped arms and chest before he was pushed sideways to cut off his circulation.

Usually by the fifth day he was afraid of falling asleep which he would do even with a book in his hand or watching television and he would let the dogs into the bedroom. There was nothing logical in believing that the presence of the dogs would keep the nightmares away just as they keep the deer and the armadillos out of the vegetable garden. But the smell of the dogs reminded him that he was a citizen of the United States who had voted in every election since 1954, that he lived at SolTerra Horse Farm in the town of Alachua, Florida, where streets were named not only after historic personalities like Martin Luther King but also after Bob Hitchcock, the benevolent grocer, and Peggy, the little engine that used to travel here not so long ago, and that he was separated only by some small woods from their son John's house and that his grandchildren would take the path through it to visit several times a day and sometimes on weekends stay as "honored guests." But the dogs couldn't keep the ghosts away for long. Scotch helped. Harvey's blended, one liter for $20 or Cluny's for

$14.59. The single malt Glenfiditch, the Christmas or birthday gift from his son, was for sipping only.

The sound of the telephone made him roll over to his wife's side of the bed to reach the receiver on the small table next to it.

"Hello," he yelled, expecting to hear Meg's voice in spite of her money-saving rule that no-news-is-good-news. Or if not Meg at least the overseas operator asking him if he would accept the charges."

"Did I wake you, Andre?"

"Charlotte! I thought it would be Meg calling. What time is it anyway?" He looked at the clock. "I should have been down at the barn feeding. The horses will have to wait for their breakfast for once."

"I'm sorry to call this early, Andre."

Charlotte was in the choir at St. Mark's. He loved her euphonic English voice. She had lived in the United States for such a long time that not even Professor Higgins could have detected a regional or a class accent.

"Have you heard from Meg yet?"

"She called when she arrived in London. When the phone rang just now I thought she'd broken her no-news-is-good-news rule."

"I wanted to call before you see it in the paper—Ed Cranmer is dead."

"Oh, no!" He was sitting on the side of the bed looking through the screen door toward the woods and the clearing used for a dressage ring where usually in the morning deer grazed but all he saw was Ed Cranmer's erect back in his red choir robe, head held high processing as if toward the altar with its lighted candles. "I can't believe it. He always seemed so healthy"

"He died at home on Wednesday. A few weeks ago he collapsed in church and was taken to North Florida Regional but he only stayed in the hospital for a day or two. We thought he was OK."

"He was my age. . . I can't believe it." He would have known if any one of their horses was sick just by looking at them at feeding times. In the past seeing Ed on Sundays processing down the aisle with the choir he would have noticed if something was wrong with him. When he and Meg left St. Mark's to start St. Charles', it had put a strain on their friendship but he could no more give up *The Book of Common Prayer* than could Charles Stuart, king and martyr in 1649. He could not accept the 1979 version that reflected the changed theology that endeavored to improve Christ and His apostles. The Book of Common Prayer had come to him fifty-two years ago as a revelation, a gift that had made whole his fractured boyhood. It happened in Todmorden, a mill-town in Lancashire where he had been sent as a European Voluntary Worker after his escape from the Communists. He was at St. Margaret's attending what he thought would be a Roman Catholic Mass, but St. Margaret's turned out to be Anglican.

"The worst thing for me," Charlotte said, "was that I learned more about Ed from his obituary than I ever knew when he was alive. Did you know that he was an actor before becoming an architect ? Or that he met his wife at a Broadway show where they were both dancers? . . . I'll call you when I know the time of the memorial service."

"Thank you. . . . He was our friend for thirty years." The words "memorial service" closed not only the curtain to signal the end of the play but also brought down a steel barrier.

* * * * * *

He was fourteen when the fourth form curriculum at the Piarist gymnasium called for an introduction to Greek

93

mythology. Their teacher, who also taught at the university, was fascinated by psychoanalysis and in his lectures had made what to the boys was an incomprehensible connection between the two. Perhaps that was the reason that he had never tried as an adult to explain even to himself what had happened on that early morning on the last day of August when, devastated by thoughts of the looming school term that would exile him to a boarding school in the city, he accompanied his mother to an early Mass at St. Theresa's where he was not only forbidden to receive the Host but was made to feel guilty, a traitor, by Dominie Barna who looked like a younger version of his Hungarian grandfather.

He and his mother were walking toward the chapel. They passed Fraulein Mitzi on her way to early Mass.

"*Guten Morgen.*"

"*Guten Morgen, Liebling*," Fraulein Mitzi said. She had been their nanny for many years. She had decided not to return to Bavaria, but to stay with them in her retirement.

There was dew on the grass. A pale-yellow sun was moving up slowly as if cranked by their old station master, Mr. Kovacs, whose duties included the raising of the gate at the railway crossing. His mother was singing *Chartres sonne, Chartres t'appelle*. In front of the rectory Fr. de Corsell was getting out of his dusty car with his black case that looked like the doctor's satchel.

"Not so loud, Mother. People can hear you."

"Just humming. *Il faut cultivar notre jardin*, Andre."

"*Laudatur*," he said, passing Fr. de Corsell.

"*In aeternum, amen*," Fr. de Corsell said, not looking at them.

"What's wrong with him?" he whispered.

"He is carrying the Reserved Sacraments, *n'est-ce pas*? Take him riding before you leave for school, Andre."

"*Oui, Maman.*"

"He *thinks* he is a good rider."

"*Tant pis.* I'll get one of the retirees from grandfather's paddock."

"*Un cheval ancien Andre,* from before 1789 if possible. Someone he can trust." They were smiling at each other. Fr. de Corsell despised the French Revolution and the nobility Napoleon had created. His family had received their title from Louis XVI.

Inside, the church was shadowy and cool. He touched the holy water in the receptacle, crossed himself and genuflected. The red sanctuary lamp glowing in the distance reminded him of the navigation lights he had seen on a boat trip to Vienna. His mother, already kneeling in a pew close to the altar turned her head and motioned for him to come forward. He walked slowly with the hesitant steps of a penitent who, burdened by sins beyond his imagination, could hardly stand upright. Then he was kneeling next to his mother inhaling the lovely, reassuring scent of St. Theresa's.

"*Benedictus qui venir in nornine Domini. Hosanna in excelsis.*" Reciting the invocation made him soar unhitched from the pull of earth's gravity. Then he heard the creaking up in the tower that always preceded the sound of the bell.

"*. . .bene dixit, fregit, deditque discipulis suis, dicens: Accipite, et manducate ex hoc omes.*"

The bell rang in measured tones. The priest elevated the Host then unexpectedly turning looked at him and said in clear French: "Je suis le pain vivant descendu da ciel. " He knew St. John's chapter six by heart in Hungarian, especially verse fifty one: "I am the living bread which came down from heaven," because Dominie Barna made him memorize it for not being attentive when "Jesus Feeding the Five Thousand" was preached.

Facing east again Fr. de Corsell still holding up the Host said, in the proper Latin of the Mass: *"Hoc Est Enim Corpus Meum."*

It was then that he saw above the altar the vision of the Infant against a white shield surrounded by tongues of fire that blocked out the cross hanging from the ceiling with the bleeding, tortured body. He was wrapped in swaddling cloth the same as the share croppers' babies but with a halo over his head, hands open, arms lifted in the beginning of an embrace. The Infant was looking at him, then laughing clapped his hands together saying: *If anyone eats of this bread he will live forever.* It wasn't said in French, Hungarian, German or any of the languages he understood. He knew then that in spite of his jumbled life he was in a state of grace. The joy he felt made him cry.

* * * * * *

Having collected the mail from his Alachua post office box he was sitting in the truck going through a bundle of bills, advertisements, and political and religious begging letters on the off chance of finding a card from Meg. Looking up he saw an old man with a trimmed beard, wearing a Creek fisherman's cap, baggy clothes and sandals walking across the parking lot. He somehow knew that the man would get into the old, boxy Volvo with the legend: "Peace starts in your kitchen. Don't eat meat," pasted on the back window. Last month waiting in the barbershop for Connie to finish working on the customer with the deeply tanned face, white forehead and rundown boots like his own, he was ready to bet that the man belonged in the new pickup with the bumper sticker: "Eat more beef." When meeting the Hare Krishnas in the library (they had a day lily nursery on the southwest end of town and a vegetarian restaurant on Bob Hitchcock's South Main Street) it was always clear who they

96

were, even the ones who spoke with New York accents. On the back window of his own pickup was the official Holsteiner Association sticker, the coat of arms of Schleswig-Holstein. He had inherited the truck from his daughter-in-law when she bought a new, more powerful one that could pull the large horse-trailer. On the back of his own car he had glued a discrete little fish. Did people file him under Approved Brother who starts every sentence with Praise the Lord or Right-wing Conspirator with barely restrained dreams of presidenticide. He often wondered about himself, wondered what had happened to the young man who once saw illuminated in the face of Christ the glory of God that had made victory over death a reality even amidst the ruins of World War II Europe. Back then in his wounded, starved body, life and death had become a hypostatic union. He felt no partiality toward either. To be with Christ in one way or the other meant peace and that was all that mattered. Now that he was coming closer and closer to the threshold where he must take off his shoes, then his garments, then all his disguises to stand naked before God where his only hope was in His Mercy, he had stopped trusting Him. He was not like an atheist denying the existence of God and the efficacy of His love. For him it was as though the Blood of the Lamb had dried leaving behind only flaking scabs. His mother had told him long ago that since the Ascension they were God's only visible representatives on earth.

"And look at us," she said once walking home after Mass.

"*Au grand serieux, Andre,* what do you see? People who hate each other." She had covered her face with her hands. "There will be another war. I can see it coming."

Five years later he was on the Eastern Front fighting the people whose writers he had studied in school, discussing their novels and plays with the Piarist Fathers. He especially thought of Dostoevsky's Brothers Karamazov, where Ivan asks his younger brother Alyosha how he could accept Christianity, accept a God whose plan involves the tears of a single child. There were thousands dying around him from starvation, bombs, artillery, executions, and machine gun fire on Easter Morning 1944 in the Ukraine. During Mass at the makeshift altar they could hear the bombers in the distance sounding like a swarm of angry bees coming toward them. There was nothing he could have said to Ivan Karamazov to change his mind without sounding hypocritical. He could only have told about Mary Magdalene recognizing the voice of her crucified, resurrected Lord. It was all he had to hold onto.

* * * * * *

The sky was a dark, rampaging river trying to drown the rooster on top of the church steeple. He had prayed only for a small flood that would cover the highway bridge leading to the city and the boarding school. The headmaster was already angry with him for helping one of the maids to hang up sheets in the attic. His sin was indelibly tattooed on his body, Domine Barna said. The water rose higher. His sister, his cousin Zoltan, his friend Otto were trying to cling to the steeple. Ed Cranmer was there too, his red choir robes flapping in the wind. Their mouths were open but there was no sound. There was no sound at all. His ears hurt from trying to hear. The heavy steel curtain of the Budapest Opera House descended. He was ashamed of himself for thinking he was old enough to stay awake through the whole Gotterdammerung. The steel curtain had become an endless wall sealing off the earth. Beyond it was suffocation. No air. Nothing. Faintly a Sanctus bell chimed and he knew he was only dreaming. It couldn't be the Sanctus bell because, that had been taken along with all the Communion vessels, altar furnishings, prayer books, hymnals,

building funds and the rectory when they were put out of St. Charles'
seven months ago.

* * * *   * *

He turned off the alarm clock. It was six o'clock, a gray morning. The three-foot-wide path the horses had worn in the dressage ring shone white in contrast to the dark grass where deer were grazing. Carefully pushing back the screen door, he lifted the binoculars. There were five deer looking like the unevenly placed dolmen he had seen with Meg in England at the Avebury prehistoric site, only these were not tombs but imperceptibly moving flesh and bone. When one of them raised its head it reminded him of the neighbor's mule. She was looking at him unblinkingly making him self-conscious, standing there wearing only a T-shirt. The breeze that moved the chimes hanging from a branch of the hickory tree swept away the gray to let the pale golden light illuminate the white flowers of the dogwood trees. He pulled off his T-shirt and waved it at the morning sky like a flag of surrender.

"All things come of Thee O Lord," he chanted.

The deer bolted noisily, churning the fallen leaves. The dogs hearing the commotion, began to bay in their various tongues. The horses were galloping in the pastures. It was March 8, Ash Wednesday.

Fear not, O land; the prophet Joel proclaimed, be glad and rejoice: for the Lord will do great things.

Standing naked in the doorway, surrounded by the flowering azaleas, dogwood and the green of the cedars like blobs of paint on an artist's palette he felt shriven like a newborn. The suffocating horror of the silence of death receded. He no longer doubted that he had been washed clean by the blood of the Lamb or that he would see wonders in the heavens and in the earth, blood, and fire, and pillars of smoke. Sixty two years ago the Infant had looked on him and said: "If anyone eats of this bread he will live forever." He was an old man now who could remember that even in the darkest horrors of war, candles were lit, the story was told, the Body was broken, and the Blood was shed to preserve his own sinful body and soul. He knew the reality of his own redemption.

The phone rang. He was certain Meg must have decided to frivolously break her no-news-is-good-news rule because she missed him. Living fifty years together makes people a necessity for each other. He reached for a towel to put around him and picked up the receiver. He knew then that in spite of his jumbled life he was in a state of grace.

The Storage Room

The kitchen door opened directly onto the middle of the screened-in back porch. To the right through an alcove another door led to the rest of the house. The doors were covered with peeling paint. The left-hand side of the porch ended in a six-by-eight-foot storage room. Its door, painted a gleaming Chinese red, stood open. A man on hands and knees was painting the floor with the same red paint. When his boots and backside became visible outside the room, the dogs, lying in the shade of the porch began moving their tails at slow windshield-wiper speed in the ninety-degree October heat, pushing around the fallen sycamore leaves. This was the end of October. In November the hickory trees would turn gold, the dogwoods and sweet gums red, but the wholesale shedding of leaves wouldn't come until December. Winter traveled at a snail's pace in north Florida.

The dogs got up, stretched, then began loping toward the invisible county road five hundred yards away. It was screened by a strand of sweet gums. He too heard the school bus now and put his paint brush in a can, then ducked through the screen door. Old Florida houses were built with high ceilings but the doors were cut for short people. The bus started off again, then the sound was blotted out by the curve in the road and he heard the dogs' happy yipping and the children's high voices. They were coming through the woods, John in the lead running with the jumping dogs who tried to lick his face. John was ten and he always ran. Sibet, at twelve, was more dignified. She walked. She was the most beautiful girl-child he had ever seen. Inside and out.

"Daddy," John shouted, "is it dry yet?"

"The door is, but the floor is still tacky I just finished it a few minutes ago."

"Daddy," Sibet said. "You'll have to talk to Johnny before he hurts himself. Mrs. McCody said that she won't allow him on her bus if he keeps on jumping about."

John was through the screen door and into the kitchen. The dogs followed him inside.

"He is really such a sweet boy, Daddy. The Cake Eaters were fighting with the Greasers on the playground and I pretended I needed his help with some school work because I didn't want him to get in any fights and he came straight away to help me."

"Darling, I don't' know who the Cake Eaters are or —"

"The Cake Eaters are the rich children. They wear different outfits every day. The Greasers are the kids who live in the country."

"Like us?"

"Johnny," Sibet burst out laughing. "Daddy thinks we are Greasers."

John appeared on the porch in a whirlwind of dogs with an apple in his hand.

"They wouldn't have us, Daddy."

"The Cake Eaters either," Sibet said. "They think we're strange."

"Why?" The pain was there again, all the names he had been called that he had unknowingly bequeathed his children, the *verfluchte Auslander*, the bloody foreigner, who might take away their jobs or want to marry their daughters.

"Why?"

"Because of you, Daddy," John said.

"He didn't mean it as it sounds, Daddy." Sibet was patting his arm. "What Johnny means is that people know you from the school auditorium when you were the foreign speaker and you told them about Christmas in Hungary."

"I like the red floor." John was peering into the storage room.

"I don't know what Mummy will think," Sibet said. "Red floorboards aren't in the best taste for a chapel."

"I found the paint under the house," he said. "I didn't buy it." Meg has good taste but she also liked to save money.

"I think it's beautiful. Sibet and I decided to call it St. Francis Chapel. Mummy will do the lettering on the door in black paint."

"We really named it for our English grandfather," Sibet said, "but we couldn't name a chapel the Reverend Edward Francis Wilkinson."

"I remember when I wanted to name my model sailboat after him and grandfather said his name belonged on the stern of a tugboat," John said. "He thought I should name my sailboat Elisabeth after grandmother."

"Are we going to visit them soon?" Sibet asked. "I love Devon and grandmother reading to us."

103

"I love scones and fireplaces," John said.

In the distance a bull started to below. Three bellows, pause, three bellows, pause.

"It sounds as if he's gone to the edge of Paynes Prairie. Would you go down, John, and see that no calves got through the fence."

"Yes, Daddy."

"And please, watch where you put your feet."

"I'm taking Brandy with me, Daddy. He goes up straight like a helicopter even if it's only an old snake skin." He began to run south, towards Paynes Prairie. All the dogs went with him.

"Could you help me in the garden, Sibet?"

"I'd rather not. I'd like to read till Mummy comes home."

"Still on the Jalna books?"

"Yes, Daddy. Renny reminds me of you."

"I'm so glad, darling." He vaguely remembered that the Renny character, besides training horses, had married his younger brother's wife.

The winter garden was in the back of the house where an external spigot made irrigation possible. The garden was surrounded by a woven sweet gum fence that belonged around an Eastern European village garden rather than a Florida one where it would rot in a few months. The man knew this, but two months ago an irrational whim had urged him to teach his children how to weave a garden fence. It made as much sense as his taking eight years of Latin at his father's urging in order to become civilized and to be able to think logically. He was thirty-seven years old now, and his emotions still came before his logical thinking. As far as the state of his civilization was concerned, Mr. Heffelfinger, one of the university's art department teachers, had told him last week—after a discussion about the place of discipline in the arts—that he was a totally uncivilized person who was not in the studio to mouth off about art since he was neither a teacher nor a student but an hourly paid model who was needed only for his hungry Arab look.

The first step in the building of the woven garden fence had been to select the right trash trees. Sweet gums grew like weeds on the place, so early on Saturday morning he and John cut down six from the thicket close to the county road, and dragged them with the tractor to the plowed garden plot behind the house. The trees were trimmed, then four of the thickest trunks were cut to the right size for the four corner posts. Next came the selection of the gate posts, the size and length of a good stout staff, then the shorter posts that held the branches that formed the fabric of the woven fence. Now, hoeing the garden, he was pleased with the artistic effect that a few weeks of sun and rain had produced. The curling bark and the silver-gray of the wood was the perfect frame for the green of the collards and radish tops, the darker greens of spinach and Swiss chard. The early, pale-green carrots resembled the thin, crew-cut hair of clowns. Beside them, four rows of English peas looked like Florentine heralds with furled flags marching toward him, their patron saint. He lifted his hoe in greeting.

"Daddy." John was trotting up to the garden surrounded by the dogs.

"Everything is all right. All the calves are around Captain Hornblower. There's a young bull on the other side of the fence. That's what he's hollering about."

A car turned onto the dirt driveway, coming through the woods.

"It's Mummy." John was running toward the front of the house. The man put down his hoe and came out of the garden feeling the peace and security of the moment. Everybody was accounted for. He went into the kitchen to boil water for their tea.

* * * * * *

"We have twenty minutes before supper," Sibet said. She closed the kitchen door behind her. Some of the dogs were lying on the porch. Brandy, who looked like an oversized brown Labrador, lay in the doorway of the chapel.

"Is Mummy coming?"

"No, Johnny. She would like to close her eyes for twenty minutes. And Brandy isn't allowed to come into the chapel even if she isn't here."

"Dogs used to come into Exeter Cathedral. Even cats," John said.

"On a leash. A sign outside said: 'Put on leash, please.'"

"I can't find Brandy's leash, Daddy."

"Just stop fussing." He closed the door behind them, noticing that somehow Brandy had ended up inside. The chapel was lovely with its gleaming red floor and curtained windows, one facing toward the country road, the other looking down on the vegetable garden. He had found the curtains in a five-and-ten; their garish roosters had originally been destined for an Early American kitchen. Meg thought the curtains in dreadful taste but the children liked them. He had been telling tales about his childhood in Hungary and the fact that he was thirteen before he had realized that the weathercock was not on their church steeple to distinguish it from the Roman Catholic church but as a symbol for the Resurrection. Three of their old steamer trunks piled on top of each other made the altar. It was covered with an old Persian carpet and on top with fair linen his mother had sent them. He made the oak cross. Meg had made the ceramic incenser that hung from the ceiling on a brass chain. The two wrought-iron candlesticks came from Mexico.

"Whose turn is it?"

"It's mine, Daddy." Sibet came to the altar, took an incense stick from a small box and put it in the incenser. "Let my prayer be set forth before thee as incense; and the lifting up of my hands as the evening sacrifice" She lit the incense stick and the candles on the altar, then went back and sat down next to her brother.

Standing beside the altar the man watched the incense rise toward the ceiling and his hands, holding the Book of Common Prayer, began to shake. He realized that God lived with them in this house.

"I acknowledge my transgressions," he read, "and my sin is ever before me."

The children went inside to set the table and wake up their mother. He stayed behind in the chapel to tidy up and clean out the incenser. When he had finished he turned off the light but the full moon keep the chapel illuminated. He stepped closer to the window and pulling aside the curtain looked out at their garden. The rows of vegetables had turned silvery, proud little knights in armor getting ready to proclaim their king. The shadow of the fence itself and his heart began to beat with a strange beat that was frightening and glorious at the same time. One of the gate posts, like Aaron's staff, had sprouted.

A week later the sprouting post bore tiny leaves the size and shape of the maple leaves around the miniature military medals his father had worn on the lapel of his tail coat on solemn occasions. Every morning after Meg and the children left, he and the dogs went in procession to the vegetable garden to look at the sprouting staff. Today he didn't have time to linger. He had to be at the art department by half-past eight and parking at the university was time-consuming and difficult.

The university painting studio was housed in one of the twenty-year-old "temporary" buildings. The floor was speckled with paint rendering the wide pine boards into a nonrepresentational Seurat. The once-white walls bore the marks of the many brushes that had been cleaned on them. The smell of turpentine reminded him of cousin Zoltan with his paint-splattered white tennis pants pushed into yellow riding boots standing in front of his easel with his head turned like a large heron to look at the model through his monocle. The easels were set up in a semicircle around a platform on which stood a cross that was constructed from a large studio easel and length of two-by-four.

"And here's Jesus," one of the students shouted, imitating Johnny Carson's announcer. There were hoots of laughter. It sounded as if he had arrived late to a cocktail party where everybody but himself was in on the joke. He went behind the battered, gilded screen and undressed. He was already wearing the fig leaf Meg had made out of a pair of blue washcloths. He stepped out from behind the screen and checked the floor for broken glass and fresh paint. Heffelfinger entered the studio.

"Good morning, ladies and gentleman. I see Mr. Jesus has already arrived. Get on your cross before I set the timer, please."

He stepped onto the platform, then onto what looked like a mounting block that would enable him to point his toes. He wanted to imitate Sir Jacob Epstein's "Risen Christ." He had seen it almost daily at St. Paul's against a temporary wall, behind which stone masons were working on damage sustained during World War II. In this image of Christ the legs were still dead, yet the head and the rest of the body were rising triumphantly. It had had a great effect on him. He was living in London illegally at that time, defying the Ministry of Labour by leaving behind Lancashire and his job in a cotton mill. He has survived by selling pencils, erasers, and postcards in front of St. Paul's.

"I have set the timer for twenty-five minutes." Mr. Heffelfinger held up the timer. "Can you see it?"

"Yes, thank you." He looked down on them, then shifted his eyes to a spot of paint on the floor to anchor himself. This way he could go away from the studio, think of Meg, the children, the dogs, the sprouting post, the hoped-for prices at the cattle market, and plan next year's planting. He wanted the studio to fade away. Even after five years, modeling still made him feel like a slab of meat.

"Our hungry Arab has classical proportions," Mr. Heffelfinger intoned. "His arms are three-and-a-half times the length of his head. His legs and torso are of equal length. You can clearly observe the muscle structure."

The pain brought him back. He tried to hold his breath to rest his back muscles but then the next deep breath hurt more. In the silence the timer ticked away. He couldn't judge how much time had passed. He couldn't control his head.

"Look at him," Mr. Heffelfinger said. "The head has fallen forward, the muscles and tendons bulge. There's hopelessness in the line of the body. This is a man dying. This is an execution. I want to see your own interpretation as long as it stands for humanism and not bigotry."

He heard the timer buzz and Heffelfinger shout: "Rest."

Two of the boys helped him down off the cross. He wasn't sure if his knees would keep him up but then the returning circulation burned through his legs and back and he was standing. The students were still at their easels, looking at him as if he were an accident victim lying in the street.

"The Crucifixion is about pain and discipline," he said, heaving like a beached fish. "It's about love. It's about the Resurrection."

"That is not, one would think, a device with a great deal of artistic mileage left in it," Heffelfinger said. "Walk around."

He walked around. Then the timer buzzed. His five-minute rest period was over. He climbed back on the cross.

* * * * * *

"The leaves are getting larger, Daddy," Sibet said. His children had beat him home. They were in the back looking at the sprouting post. The dogs were there too, lying halfway under the house. The temperature had gone up to eighty-two even though the hickory trees, the dogwoods, and the sweet gums had changed into their November costumes.

"I told Jimmy Sapp that we were given a sign," John said. "He's a Baptist."

"He told some of the other boys too," Sibet said.

"Then we can expect a phone call from the ACLU any minute now," the man said.

The leaves had grown to the size of a quarter. He imagined the people who would come to touch the tree and pray in the chapel but them remembered that Mr. Bardsley had told them that they could rent the land and the house as long as he lived but then the property would be sold to a developer. Mr. Bardsley was old and sickly. After he died, the house—it had been an antique shop in town before it was moved and not one of the doors or windows fitted—would be bulldozed and with it the chapel and the tree.

"Do you know why Aaron's staff sprouted?"

"For a sign," John said.

"A sign for what?"

"That he and his brother could trust God," Sibet said.

Two nights later, when the moon was blotted out by a black cloud and the wind rattled the rusty tin roof of their house he awoke, rose from his bed being careful not to wake Meg, and padded out to the kitchen. One of the windows looked out

110

toward the vegetable garden but he couldn't see anything in the dark. On and off the wind played with the roof and made the trees sigh, then it stopped and he could hear the dogs scratch themselves under the house. He opened the refrigerator and by its light took out salami, margarine, green peppers, and bread and began to eat, but because he was naked, the food didn't taste right. He got a towel from the bathroom and draped it round his waist. When he had finished eating, he went through the kitchen door to the back porch and outside. The wind blew up again making the roof sound like a snare drum. The dogs came out from under the house and licked his legs but he pushed them away.

He sat down on the ground by the sprouting post thinking that he was a dirt farmer who owned only an Angus bull he had raised from a calf and fifteen mixed-breed beef cows with calves at their sides on forty acres of rented land. That was all. During the last five years the only outside job he had been able to get was as a model hanging from a cross or slowly rotating while trying to remember art history illustrations so that he could assume a different pose every five minutes. He wasn't like the other husbands and fathers with their real jobs and paychecks.

He rested his forehead against the post conjuring up scenes of the people who would sit under the post-grown-into-a-tree, enveloped in a cocoon of heavenly peace. They would all help to buy the place and turn it into a retreat center. He had always wanted to be a part of something like the Lee Abbey Fellowship, in Lynton, North Devon, where the homeless could get back their strength for a year or two before going out into the world to try again, where unwed mothers and their newborns would have an accepting, living family, where the sick could recuperate or die in peace, where everybody would be fed.

It was then that the moon swallowed the black cloud and the distended face glared down on the sprouting post and he saw the black spots on the new leaves, some already dry and shriveled. The shock that hit him was as brutal as if he had been a workman whose collapsed scaffolding had hurled him to the ground to break all the bones in his body. He knew that in this fallen world people had been predestined to pain and loss and death. He wanted to shield his children from this knowledge. The water spigot was between the kitchen and the chapel windows. He filled the watering can and began to water the sprouting post.

By the next day all the lovely, delicate leaves had turned into a soot-like substance that the slightest puff of wind would blow away as if they and the blackened stems had become illustrations of an eschatological discussion on the corruption of all life. When he told the children about the death of the sprouting post they said they already knew. They had noticed the dried up leaves but hadn't wanted to upset him.

At seven o'clock he went into the chapel to prepare for Evensong. Brandy was already under the children's wagon-bench, which had been purchased specifically for the chapel at a flea market.

"It isn't fair to the other dogs," Meg said, coming in with the children. They could hear the jingle of rabies tags as the other dogs scratched themselves on the back porch.

"Brandy is the only one who is really interested in coming into the chapel, Mummy," John said. He lit the candles on the altar, ignited the stick of incense, then sat down on the bench.

"Repent ye; for the Kingdom of Heaven is at hand," the man read, standing by the side of the altar, wondering if the Kingdom would turn out to be a burned-out place like his home after the war. In their garden the leaves of the trees had been blown down by the blast and a puff of air that was stirring them about on his scattered inheritance.

They all knelt down.

"Almighty and most merciful Father; We have erred and strayed from thy ways like lost sheep." He was looking at Meg and the children kneeling with closed eyes, John's left hand reaching back under the wagon-bench, touching Brandy's head. They didn't look like lost sheep. They looked like God's own lambs. "And grant, O most merciful Father, for his sake; That we may hereafter live a godly, righteous, and sober life, To the glory of thy holy Name."

"Amen."

"Our Father, which art in heaven . . ." He watched the incense rise, their prayer joining with the larger Church, and he thought of his father-in-law, a clerk in Holy Orders, who had given him the Book of Common Prayer whose text had been in use for five hundred years but had been discarded now in favor of one produced by a committee of tone-deaf people in the name of progress. "The power, and the glory, For ever and ever."

"Amen." They stood.

"O Lord, open thou our lips," he chanted, hearing his father-in-law's voice as it had sounded in countless Devonshire village churches.

"And our mouth shall shew forth they praise."

"O God, make speed to save us."

"O Lord, make haste to help us."

"Praise ye the Lord."

"The Lord's Name be praised."

Sibet handed John the Bible open at the proper place. The boy stepped to the other side of the altar and turned. (*He that readeth so standing and turning himself, as he may be best heard of all such as are present.*)

113

"Here beginneth the third chapter of the book of Habakkuk," the boy said. "A prayer of Habakkuk the prophet."

He loved his son's voice. It made it possible for him to accept the fact that for the rest of his life he would speak with an accent no matter which language he spoke.

"Lord, I have heard of your fame; I stand in awe of your deeds, O Lord. Renew them in our day, in our time make them known."

It was as if the man had been jolted with electricity that was too much for his body to absorb and he reached out to hold on to the altar for support to endure the intense silver light that banished all the shadows and showed the shabbiness of the storage room. He felt naked, and insignificant, dependent like a little child and he saw God's Kingdom visible even in this storage room and he understood that signs were not given to be embalmed, shown off, or guarded like the poor god-manqué in the glass case in the Kremlin; they were posted for the benefit of the weak and shortsighted who had lost their way.

"The Sovereign Lord is my strength; he makes my feet like the feet of a deer, he enables me to go on the heights," the boy finished the reading. "Here endeth the first lesson."

He couldn't wait any longer. "Did you see..."

"Yes, Daddy," Sibet said. "We all know that when two or three are gathered..."

The dogs began to bark and then they heard a car pull up to the front porch. Now the dogs gave tongue as if they had already treed the car. Brandy was whining to get out. The car horn beeped.

"They are afraid to leave the car," he said. "I'd better go and see what they want."

It took him a half-hour to convince the three slightly drunk fraternity brothers and their girlfriends that he didn't have pot to sell. What one of their friends had seen was not a marijuana patch but an experimental plot of kenaf he was growing for the university's Institute of Food and Agricultural Sciences. Kenaf was an Asiatic plant of the mallow family. The researchers hoped that its fiber could be used for paper making. He offered to take them to his kenaf patch but they were not interested.

Prices were good in January, especially for grass-fed beef that was in fashion now. They had always produced lean beef because they couldn't afford corn to feed them out. Their winter garden had produced till the middle of February when they started planting for the summer. Mr. Bardsley had died before the first plant showed. By the end of March the bulldozers were on the place marking out the streets and lots that a sign declared to be THE HUNTERS GLEN. The kenaf experiments had been permanently discontinued, but he was offered at temporary proofreading job in the editorial department of the University of Florida's Institute of Food and Agricultural Sciences, with the prospects for a permanent position in the future. By April, they had scraped together enough for a down payment on a fenced fifteen-acre parcel "planted to Bahia grass" on the edge of town. There was a "livable" shack on the place and a small storage shed.

A Book of Amos

At first it signified nothing that the rural electric company had come to prune the sycamore on the right of their entrance drive. He would have kept on loving the majestic tree—planted years ago to be one side of an arch envisioned before the bare root slip of a tree was in the ground—even though it had been turned into a freshly clipped poodle. His wife's dislike of the grotesque and his own acceptance of her taste brought an onslaught of yellow trucks and assorted machinery the next day. The largest truck pulled a two-wheel trailer carrying a machine resembling the severed head of an elephant. The tree was cut down, its branches fed into the elephant's mouth to be spat through its trunk into the truck. The sliced-up tree trunk was lifted piece by piece into another truck. After the crew nailed back the busted horse fence, they departed.

It was later, at lunch time, that he noticed the phlox that grew in the swale had been rubbed out by the yellow machines and trucks, leaving behind a muddy, oozing scar. These were the phlox he had collected from the verge of a highway destined for widening. First they had become bouquets decorating their oak dining room table and the mantel over the fireplace. The mantel still smelled the same as when he and his son had felled the cedar to make room for the house. When the phlox were dry he simply put them down in rows in the swale that made them look like victims laid out after a bombardment or some devastating natural disaster, but by the time the highway construction was finished the phlox in their swale had become a magic carpet.

Cutting down the other sycamore—his granddaughter Kate's climbing tree, the left side of the arch—was a logical thing to do, yet he had attempted to rationalize the act, blaming it on the roots interfering with the vegetable garden.

His trees were not Amos's sycamore-fig trees. He was not a shepherd like the seer. He only looked after thoroughbreds in training for dressage and stadium jumping on the land that was in his name but that he knew belonged to God, who was directing the succession of moments in his life toward a predetermined goal that allowed him to see God's glory and at the same time to understand the horrors of the way stations of his life. Forty-six years ago he had worked in a Lancashire mill town as a twentieth-century indentured weaver—part of the flotsam of World War II and communism—where a people frightened of losing their four pounds sterling weekly wages (barely enough to keep them in tea, bread, fish and chips, and coal) took away his humanity by turning him into an invisible man who would become visible only for a short time to some women in the dark on Saturday nights.

Standing under the big Florida sky, hearing the horses contentedly munching their feed, he knew that sometimes the sacred overlapped the profane to allow him to see the beauty of

God. At those moments the smells and sounds of the cotton mills and the hurt that lived in his memory like a badly healed wound were surrounded by a love that had the power to transform pain into a pearl of priceless possession.

Only fifteen miles from their farm, the university town was a microcosm of the changing West with its decaying spiritual vision reflected in the art gallery displays, where artists dispensing with perspective and iconography rendered the world and all life therein hammered flat like a character in a Dylan Thomas poem. Footprints of the reductive analytic method of psychology were everywhere in every phase of life that tried in the process to destroy the world of the spirit and with it the Judeo-Christian perception of reality that assigned moral choices to the individual.

Many of the teachers of religion and literature adopted theories that instead of bringing enlightenment handed explosives to their students because they didn't have the imagination to see what this would do to a culture two thousand years in the making. Lacking the understanding and courage of a Sigmund Freud, who seeing the final vista of his search took his own life, they followed the trail of his reductive ideas to the bitter end, where crabs were "not lower or less complex than human beings in any meaningful way," as the Marxist biologist of the Smithsonian put it. They didn't understand that a universe devoid of a standard for truth ushered in the death of any significant exchange between people. All discussions could be stopped now with: "That is your opinion." Like midway barkers promising that "everything will be shown, everything will be revealed," the lack of common standards, and research fueled by politics and social fashions, produced scientific findings in support of the feminist theory that human behavior is not caused by unchangeable biological factors, while at the same time and by the same discipline proved that biology does not allow choice for the homosexual.

Amos, who was not a prophet nor a prophet's son but a simple herdsman and a dresser of sycamore trees, knew better. "Do horses run upon rocks?" he had asked. "Does one plow the sea with oxen? Does a snare spring up from the ground, when it has taken nothing?" Those who proclaimed an absolute truth were judged obscene, and were forbidden to speak on university campuses, the same campuses that invited speakers advocating the killing of "men, women, children, the blind, and the cripple" of the wrong color or religion. Only fifty years after the Holocaust, demonstrating against that proclamation was called "hysterical" by a student newspaper.

On Valentine's Day, TV news showed snowstorms in New York. In north Florida people who lived on the land planted Irish potatoes. Feeding the horses in the morning he felt a spring breeze that was like a touch of God. Valentine's Day wasn't a postal holiday and in the afternoon he collected a letter that had come all the way from Lancashire, from his one and only cotton-mill friend who had gone on to study philosophy on a scholarship at Lancaster University. Through the years, they had kept up an intermittent correspondence about their lives, philosophy, God, growing leeks, suicide, pain, and love that, according to his friend John, were entwined. They didn't agree on many things, except for the superiority of Florida's weather over the freezing cold and lashing horizontal rains of Lancashire.

"My beliefs," John wrote, "contain what can be described as scientific candor, i.e., that beliefs cannot be entertained unless there is some objectively verifiable evidence, or a set of hypotheses that can be articulated which can show the theory to be false. To me a hypothesis, to be worthy of consideration, must be falsifiable."

120

He was reading the letter standing under the large hickory tree that he had surrounded with small limestone boulders in memory of the hut circles he had seen on the English moors.

And God said: "It's time for you to speak."

The dogwood and wild plums were covered with white lace mantillas. Red and pink azalea buds glowed like fairy lights against the backdrop of the rough-cut cedar siding of their house.

And God said: "Go and speak the Truth." He was afraid, knowing that he had an accent, that he stuttered when he was anxious. He was not the kind of person God should be sending anywhere.

The pink banner—actually several banners fastened together—attached to a second story window of Library East bisected the Park of the Americas and was anchored at the other side to a second story window of the chemistry building. Because of its length the banner sagged, creating an impression of a sinkhole drawing the foot-high letters of its messages into it. The messages began with a crude drawing of a church with a crooked cross on its steeple.

> This old house of patriarchy has got to come down;
> Our Maker Sophia we are women in your image;
> Don't let your wombs be colonized;
> Don't let Jesus marginalize us;
> God is an abusive parent;
> Call Protective Services.

He was standing, a big, gray-headed man, somewhere under the middle of the banner where the words seemed to drip on his head like some newfangled torture, watching students and professors unconcernedly walking about, seeing the Hare Krishnas, many of them Children of the Promise who had forsaken the God of Abraham, Isaac, and Jacob, beating on tambourines that reminded him of his first meeting with the

Salvation Army at the Leeds bus station in England, where he was moved to give what was left of his week's paycheck. He was looking at the banner not seeing it because he was crying. Neither did he hear the shouted slogans of a group of women nearby. He lifted his arms as if in prayer.

"All of you people listen to me," he called over the sound of the tambourines, the noise of the Frisbee players, the barking dogs, the slogan-shouting women.

"The Sovereign Lord declares: 'The days are coming when I will send a famine through the land—not a famine of food or a thirst for water, but a famine of hearing the words of the Lord.' "

He watched the women begin to march toward him like a Roman legion in its battle squares, saw two campus police officers talking into their walkie-talkies moving toward him.

"'People will stagger from sea to sea and wander from north to east, searching for the word of the Lord, but they will not find it.'"

He felt spittle mingling with his tears. The police officers were running toward him. A Frisbee like a black sun hung suspended over his head.

Before the Mountains Were Born

The spring sunlight came through the clouds, illuminating the woods, turning the shadows into faint, artistic shadings. One of the horses snorted, then with one accord they all moved, flowing in a gentle "S" toward the open pasture, their hooves beating a triumphant drum roll. There was a young redbud planted between the grey cypress house and the woods. Sitting on the porch looking at it he remembered his mother saying that buds were sealing wax with springs' coat of arms pressed on them.

It didn't seem so fanciful here in Florida. There was a natural proscenium between the lawn and the edge of the woods. Beyond it stood a strangely shaped dogwood, an antlered beast from *A Midsummer Night's Dream* wreathed with white blossoms. A bird feeder suspended between two bare hickory trees swung from side to side; the birds and squirrels were underneath pushing and shoving. One squirrel on top of the bird feeder was watching him.

"Ronald is looking at me," he said to the screen door. "I can't ignore him, Meg."

"Don't you dare, Jeremy. We agreed that he has to live with the other squirrels if he's going to have a chance."

"He thinks I am his father." Ronald was hanging by his hind legs from the top of the bird feeder, stuffing his mouth with little black hands. On the ground under the feeder the squirrels and birds were eating the seeds Ronald was shaking down.

"You're too old to be his father." Meg came out on the porch and sat down next to him. He always wondered how she remained so slim and beautiful, white hair and all.

"And, seriously, most people are not pleased when a wild creature jumps on their shoulders."

Ronald had been such a sweet little squirrel nesting in a discarded Easter basket like a baby Moses, drinking his formula from a dolls bottle every two hours. Nobody was afraid of him then. They had named him after Megs Uncle Ronald, an Anglo-Catholic priest who died on the day they had found Ronald.

"Ronald!" he clapped his hands. The chipping sparrows flew up in a ground-level explosion and the squirrels ran. A brown and black dog—a mixture of basset and dachshund—partly hidden by the honeysuckle on the porch banister, beat the floorboards with his tail.

"Ralphie is pleased with life," Meg said.

"So am I." The hills didn't skip like lambs, but even so he recognized the favor of the Lord. "I think I'll go to Cursillo," he said. "Every time I see the Shubs they ask me to."

"I don't think you should, Jeremy. From what I gather it isn't something for you."

"How do you know?"

"I see enough. Thirty years in psychology gives one some idea about techniques. I don't think you should go."

"It would mean so much to Chuck and Marian," he said. "It would really make them happy." The breeze that always came from the southeast in the spring made the white dogwood petals float like confetti.

* * * * * *

They stopped at a hamburger joint on the way to Jacksonville. There was a three-quarter-size statue of a Brahman bull in the parking lot. He liked the Brahman breed. Their long ears and sweet faces reminded him of Pinocchio after he had been turned into a donkey. His own herd bull had been a Black Angus named after C. S. Forester's Captain Horatio Hornblower. He felt silly reading the Hornblower series at his age, but when the first book was published in America he had been a Hungarian teenager whose escape reading was Greek mythology.

"Supper is on us," Chuck said.

"That's very kind of you." The red checkered tablecloth could have covered a table in any of Budapest's "summer" restaurants with their glinting fairy-lights. "I wish you didn't have to go to all this trouble to get me to Jacksonville. I don't know why I couldn't drive myself."

"Trust us," Marian said. "We are your sponsors. It's a great joy for us."

"Where in Jacksonville are we going?"

"You don't need to know," Chuck said.

"Can't you tell me anything about it?"

"The whole retreat is built on trust and love," Marian said. "Trust us."

"You'll be leaving me there for three days!"

"It's only two nights," Chuck said. "Let's order."

* * * * * *

He leaned into a corner of the back seat, with eyes closed, listening to the sound of the Shubs' voices in front forming an intimate, closed circle. It was dark outside. He wondered if Meg was eating her supper alone or had perhaps decided to walk across their woods to eat with the children. He himself had been unable to eat. He had only had a cup of black coffee.

The car slowed to a stop, then accelerated going in a wide circle entering I-10.

"Not much longer now," Chuck said over his shoulder. He didn't answer, pretending to be asleep, letting his body roll with the motion of the car. To cope with fear he had taught himself suspended animation on Christmas Eve in '43. The Kiev power plant had just been blown up again. This time by the Red Army, not the Germans. He had been ordered on arrival at the train station to supervise the unloading of tanks (they were Panzer IVs with 7.5 cm. main armament plus 2 MG 34's), then to report to the aid station to receive his third typhus shot. While he waited he watched the wounded being brought in. Most of the tank crews had hideous, charred faces and hands, and hair that looked like blackened grass. Still waiting two hours later, he saw a doctor in a bloody apron rush out of the operating room yelling.

"I always tell them not to stuff themselves. They get hit and their stomach explodes and there is nothing I can do . . . Understand? Nothing. An empty stomach would have only a little hole. A little hole."

He watched the doctor turn on his heel and rush back into the operating room. As the door swung open the smell of blood and excrement descended on him like a low cloud on top of a

126

mountain. He closed his eyes to ward off the smell and thought of home, of Hungary, of their summer house, and saw Mitzi the komondor—named after one of their former nannies, a white-haired German woman—lying in a triangle of sunlight on the clay floor that led into the wine cellar, her white fur blown gently by the breeze, and he felt his own limbs relax as if on a summer morning at the beginning of a school holiday.

"Are you sick or wounded, lieutenant?" A corpsman was standing in front of him.

"Neither. Thank you." He stood up and left the hospital. He never did get his third typhus shot.

"You can't imagine the welcome you'll get," Marian said.

They left I-10 at the Church Street exit.

* * * * * *

The large hall was lit by strong, overhead lights. People were rushing all over, greeting each other. Luggage moved on trolleys. He was standing in front of a table.

"Welcome to Men's Cursillo #7, Jeremy." The man sitting behind the table looked like an immigration official. The Shubs embraced him and were gone. Somebody took his saddlebag that held toiletries, tobacco, pipe, bootjack, and knife on one side, and underwear, socks, and shirts on the other. The man behind the table wrote down his name, then stood up and embraced him as if he were sending him on a long sea voyage. When they finally left, it wasn't to embark on the SS *Washington* or one of the *Queens*: They were herded onto a yellow school bus.

* * * * * *

A tree branch scraped the roof and screeched down the whole length of the bus. He could hear the wheels slipping on the loose dirt road and the muted roar of the city in the distance sounding like a giant wave rolling after them. When they had left what he now thought of as the replacement depot, all the men were talking and joking at the top of their voices. In his experience it was always like this; first the loud corny jokes, then confidences in case—dying was still only an intellectual possibility for the new replacements—then when gunfire was clearly gunfire and not distant thunder all talk ceased and the veterans like him knew that they were back where they belonged. Reality was never as bad as their imagination.

The bus stopped next to three other yellow school buses. Dim lights were strung among the trees. Beyond the trees he could see the barracks.

"A through G," somebody shouted. "Line up. Your luggage is waiting for you in your designated building."

"H through P."

"Q to Z."

They lined up. To one side was a building that looked like an HQ with its communications gear, though he knew that it was only a TV antenna. He entered the A through G building and saw his saddlebag on a lower bunk by one of the walls. The man sitting next to it looked at the label, then at him.

"Are you Jeremy?" The man stood up. "I hope you like a lower bunk."

"Yes, thank you."

"Take off your watch."

He began to sweat, feeling the wetness spreading down his side.

"Your watch," the man said.

He was looking at the alligator emblem on the man's polo shirt. A watch wasn't worth dying for, he thought, remembering people who did because they were too slow to hand over theirs. He extended his hand, dangling the watch from it like a dead fish.

"No, no," the man said. "just put it away. Here we depend on the bell. The first evening you'll be under the rule of silence." The man left and he sat down on the bunk bed listening to his heart slap, slap, slap as if he had a trained seal inside his chest. He watched the others lie down on their beds or quietly walk about. It was always the same in camps. The first rule was to orient oneself.

He hid his watch under the socks in his saddlebag. Then he opened the other side, pulled out his knife, and thrust it into the top of his right boot.

* * * * * *

What he had taken for an HQ building turned out to be the dining hall where they spent most of the morning sitting around tables in small groups listening to talks given by men who sounded as though they had memorized canned speeches on "Piety," on "Laity," on "Ideal," on "Study," on "Action." There was to be no discussion. The leader—his official title was "rector"—said, "I want you to remember each talk exactly as you heard it. We are not interested in your opinion about them. We know what we are doing. Trust us."

At his own table, the other six men, his brothers in Christ from the Diocese of Florida, were taking notes.

"I am not about to memorize crap," he said. "I haven't heard so much bad theology in my whole life."

"That's not the right attitude," Fred said. He was the unofficial leader of their group. "You've been bitching all morning. You and that priest behind us."

The bell ringer walked through the dining hall looking like an anxious town crier. The polite silence of the hall was transformed into a loud buzz and laughter. Outside, the spring sunlight lit up the green grass. It had been burned to speed up the greening process, but here and there were the charred remains of the winter grass. In the distance among the trees he saw the sun glinting on a chain-link fence and watched Fred scurrying toward the staff housing. There was always a spy, a spionka, reporting to the staff. Usually the criminal among the political prisoners.

He bent down, touched the top of his right boot to feel his knife, then lay down on the grass, letting his body float up to the blue sky.

* * * * * *

They returned to a transformed, festive dining. hall. The tables were set and adorned with vases of flowers. There were balloons flying from the backs of chairs.

"Everybody line up against the walls," a young priest said, "so that we encircle the hall."

"Reach for your brothers hand."

He felt their combined strength and thought of Jericho, all their own individual Jerichoes and all the walls that would tumble down to set them free to love God and each other.

"You all know the Edelweiss tune. I want you to sing the blessing to that tune. One . . . two . . . three."

They began to sing, hesitatingly at first, then someone began to sway from side to side until all of them were swaying like drunken Bavarians at an Octoberfest. The priest pulled up his right trouser leg, showing his drooping sock, and began to kick, first the right leg, then the left, in a slow parody of a chorus line. Somebody whooped, and soon there was a chorus line all around the walls bellowing the sickly sweet tune. He let go of the hands he was holding and stepped away. It embarrassed him to look at them as if looking at them would turn him into a Peeping Tom to emphasize his foreignness that could not understand when fun was fun and when it was bad taste. He felt guilty because he really didn't want to join in.

* * * * * *

The food was good and there was plenty of it. Nobody sat with arms encircling their plates shoveling food into their mouths as if filling sandbags to hold back a flooded Styx. There were no corpses in this camp with skin and bones for buttocks, but he knew he shouldn't have come. He was like an alcoholic plunked down in the middle of a bar surrounded by sounds and smells that triggered memories. He heard the sound of men crying, men separated from their families, crying because they knew there was no way out. They always moved them as soon as the transport was made up.

"These are for you, Jeremy." One of the kitchen staff handed him a packet of envelopes.

"Thank you." He was not hallucinating. Men really were crying. "Where did these letters come from?" There were no postal markings on the envelopes.

"Find out."

He opened the first envelope.

"Dear Jeremy,"

"Our prayers have been with you daily since you decided to make your Cursillo. It is really neat and it makes us so happy that

131

you are joining us. So, please relax, now, and just let God do his thing."

"We know it is a fantastic and humbling experience to see Christ in the faces of your brothers there and our palanca for you is prayer and fasting. Daily prayers and fasting by giving up one meal a day for the past week. We have made altar visits on your behalf and our thoughts and prayers are with you now. De Colores!"

"Chuck and Marian"

Each word was written in a different color ink.

"My mom wrote," Chris, the youngest man at their table, said. "She says she loves me. She misses me." He was crying.

There was nothing he could say to Chris. He shuffled the envelopes. On one of them he recognized Megs handwriting. He knew that they were being manipulated, but he couldn't stop crying. He looked up. Fred was watching him with clinical interest.

* * * * * *

"Wake up, Jeremy."

He pretended to be sleeping to gain time to sort out the sounds around him.

"Jeremy."

"I am up." Fred was bending over him. It was still dark outside. "Isn't it too early to get up?"

"The others are all outside."

"All right."

"You can't go out in shorts."

"All right." If they took you out in your shorts it meant that you would be shot in a ditch. Ditches were easy to cover over. He pulled on his jeans, socks, boots and waited for the command to

132

pick up his saddlebag. It meant that he'd be on the next transport.

"Let's go, Jeremy."

"O.K." He wasn't told to pick up his saddlebag. It didn't make any sense. There was no logic to it. His knife was in the back pocket of his jeans. He touched, it to make sure.

* * * * * *

In the grey light the faces were dirty-white blobs, the mouths black holes. They were singing, standing three deep separated by a few feet of black chasm. Then the singing stopped and there were the shouted names and he remembered the fence that divided them at the transit camp at Ujpest: on the outside, mothers, fathers, wives, children, sweethearts, brothers, sisters, friends, neighbors who through a miraculous grapevine had found out where they had been taken and had come to shout their names. On the inside were the prisoners, some of whom had been factory workers six hours ago and were picked up on their way home to make up the missing numbers in the prisoner-of-war count. There was always the interminable counting of prisoners. The numbers had to tally with a predetermined total as if the Bolshevik Revolution at heart was nothing more than a double-entry book keeping system preoccupied with the right count even if it meant taking some of the surviving Hungarian Jews with yellow stars still on their breasts or uniformed Hungarian postmen stopped in the middle of their rounds.

The morning light took away the chasm that had been only a shadow cast by the singers. People were embracing and those on the inside were crying as if they had been in for years when in reality it had been only two days. He heard his name called. Marian Shub, then Chuck and others, men and women he knew

133

only slightly from diocesan conferences, embraced him. Everybody was talking and laughing. The fog, backlighted by the sun, produced a washed-out photograph as if somebody had set off a giant flashbulb to freeze them in an embrace forever.

Soon the visitors were leaving, waving their arms in farewell, moving away with slow steps that resembled a formal dance. He followed them.

"You shouldn't go beyond this point." A tall, thin priest stepped out from behind a large magnolia tree. "We rented this place from some Roman Catholic monks who train police dogs. If you walk by the kennels and set them off it will be hours before they can quiet them down."

"Thank you." He waited, listening for the dogs' bark. The visitors had gone beyond the critical point. The dogs were not barking. Something was wrong. He had to get out.

Up the rise toward the tree line. There were no guard towers. This wasn't a permanent camp. There were no guard towers.

"Hey, fella . . . where d'you think you're going?"

He heard the guard shouting. Remembering, his back muscles tensed, waiting to hear the click before being hit, then he was behind a tree, lying on his stomach, watching the guard. The next minute he was squatting under a table where he always squatted in a recurring nightmare. The table was in a cheap dive on the Pest side of Budapest where he had pawned his father's cigarette case, the square silver one with the enamel crest, the last of his father's presents. He squatted, smelling the Russians and the spilled wine, hearing Meg and the children asking why he wasn't coming home. Then his dogs howled, some caught in traps in Florida pine woods, some waiting in ditches with broken legs. One old collie who was terrified of water was floating in an unfinished swimming pool filled with rainwater. He couldn't move to help her. He was surrounded by the Russian soldiers' short, scuffed boots.

"Hey, fella . . . where d'you think you're going?"

He heard the Russian shout again. He crawled away circling to get close to him, then stood up, momentarily blacking out. He was standing behind a large hickory tree, sweating, and shaking, holding his knife in his right hand, staring at the cassock-clad back of his own priest.

* * * * * *

At eleven o'clock they received Communion. The chapel was a dingy little room with rows of plywood flip-up chairs from an old movie house and a wooden altar with a metal cross on it. The lamp was lit and it glowed reassuringly in the glum interior. He could smell the wine and the Prayer Books, then he heard the words and was filled with thankfulness for the presence of God who stood with them in spite of their sins; the Presence whose grace was sufficient for all of them.

* * * * * *

The school bus pulled into a church parking lot filled with cars though there were no people to be seen as if the service had already started. They had not, as he expected, come back to the building they had started off from on Friday evening. The church was built of white stone in the Florida-Spanish style of the '20s. They marched under a white arch with painted sky-blue spandrels whose pristine beauty made him feel dirtier than he actually was, a soldier returning from a lost war made more visible by his uniform. He noticed a man watching them from the parking lot, but he was too spent emotionally to react. This morning he had put his knife in the saddlebag. What made him so tired and afraid was the energy he had had to expend to stay still behind the hickory tree when all that he knew, all that he had experienced, told him to use the knife.

They marched in a column toward the closed church door. He was wondering when they would go home, remembering other homecomings and other "returnees". He knew from experience that another counting would commence as soon as they stopped. The more he thought about it the worse it got. I am here, he thought. He remembered his friend Paganini, the ex-U.S. Navy pilot who, when the need arose, docked destroyers without the help of tugboats in Spain and at Guantanamo. Paganini had taught him to navigate.

"The U.S. Navy is never lost," Paganini had said. "They always know where they are."

"How come?"

"Navigation."

"Would you teach me?"

"Certainly. First you look up at the sky."

"Does it have to be at night?"

"No. It can be at any time. . . . O.K. You look up at the sky. Then you look down at the deck under your feet and say, 'I am here.' " Paganini laughed. "See how easy it is?"

The watcher they had seen earlier at the parking lot opened the church door from the inside. I am here, he thought, I am here, and stepped over the threshold. He was looking toward the altar and the rose window above it, at the light pouring in between the hardwood mullions forming a circle of eternity. He saw the lamp and from memory deep inside him he heard the chanting: "Sanctus, Sanctus," amplified by soaring walls. "Sanctus."

"God is in his holy temple," he thought. "Let all the earth be silent before him."

* * * * * *

The sound came so suddenly that it transformed itself into an optical illusion of a kaleidoscope rotated with manic speed that rendered both "kalos" and "eidos" nonexistent and turned him into a doubly endangered species threatened on one side by a hierarchy that wanted to sink biblical authority into a sea of brothers and sisters whose clapping hands and campfire songs beamed their love for Jesus and for him, blundering about like good-natured, shortsighted elephants, not noticing that they had not left even standing room for anybody else. He remembered Exeter Cathedral where, besides the people and a ginger cat, the church mouse also had a tiny entrance in the appropriate Gothic style.

"You and I are going up together," Chris whispered to him.

"What for?" The camp returnees all sat together. Their bishop entered, intensifying the clapping and singing.

"To witness about it. About Cursillo."

"Did you like it? The camp and all that?"

"It changed my life," Chris said.

He was denied all that the others received, that made them cry and sway and sing, as if his foreignness or something in him set him apart, kept him on the outside. Where was home?

"It's our turn now," Chris said. They left their pew. At the lectern they turned around and he saw his brethren, their arms stretched up, swaying like sago palms in a breeze.

"Cursillo has changed my life," Chris was saying, still fighting tears. "When I read my mother's letter it was the first time that I

137

ever saw it written down that she loved me and I understood Jesus' love for me."

"Neat," the bishop said. "Isn't that neat!"

Where was home, he thought, where? He looked at his brethren, their swaying arms, their happy, shining faces, Meg sitting among them as if her civilized presence would mediate all that was wrong with him. People were clapping and laughing and praising God, waiting for him to relax and speak, to let God do his thing through him. A terrible shroud-like solitude enveloped him standing there between the altar and the congregation, a piece of ground that for him had become a no-mans-land to be shot at from all sides. He turned, looking toward the altar and the rose window above it, at the light pouring in between the hardwood mullions forming a circle of eternity, and he remembered his home, his everlasting, unmovable inheritance. He had known God some 60-odd years, but God had known him always.

He turned back toward his brethren, seeing their happy, excited faces, their uplifted arms.

"I received Communion," he said. "I am always grateful to receive Communion."

Transformations

At the entrance, to the left of the cash register, stood a dark cherry china cabinet whose elaborate carvings imitated the pulsating fins of a tropical fish. The cabinet held only a few objects: a dark gray rock, a porcelain figurine, and a small plant. These objects were repeated like a visual mantra by mirrors and a hidden light. Next to the cabinet a four-foot carving of a carp stood on its tail.

There was a pleasant fragrance that could not readily be associated with cooking. The presence of a short, chunky waiter with slicked-back black hair and almond-shaped eyes transformed even that slight odor into the incense of sandalwood, the mystery of the Orient. The waiter, standing with his back to the dining room under an arch of dark, dragon-carved mahogany, was gazing through the window at the reality of the town where the University of Florida and its Fighting Gators pervaded every aspect of life. It was ten minutes past one. The lunchtime crowd had receded like an outgoing tide. There was only a gray-headed couple left in one of the booths, facing each other over the paper-strewn table.

"It's very simple," the woman said. She jotted down numbers on the paper in front of her. "Add your retirement income to your social security check."

"Meg thinks that if I retire we'll have to march hand in hand into an almshouse," the man said. The woman smiled.

"I doubt if it will come to that. You'll be earning only about a hundred dollars a month less than you do now. Did her own retirement make that much difference in your finances?"

"I don't know. She's the one who writes the checks and pays the bills. But I'm glad that she retired. Our twenty acres is a family compound-cum-horse-farm. She really loves looking after the grandchildren. She missed out on our own when they were little. She went out to work and I was elected to stay home."

"I think that's why you feel guilty about retiring. You want to prove you can be the main breadwinner and let her stay home with the children," the woman said.

"You may be right. House husbands were not 'in' at that time. But it was easier for Meg to get a job. Psych. O.T.'s were always in demand. I did work nights as a hospital orderly. We both believed that one parent should stay with the children till they were at least four years old. My sister and I had a German nanny who spanked us in the bathtub. We never told our parents. Children accept almost anything that grownups do."

"Well, anyway," the woman said, "according to these figures dealing only with your income, you can retire. If you want to wait till '92 you'll have twenty eight years for your state retirement. This September you'll have twenty seven years, but your pension will be almost the same amount." She pushed the paper across the table for him to see.

140

"I still have two payments left on the car."

"There is no law, Andre, that says you can't use your retirement income for car payments. Your house and land are paid for and you are sixty seven years old."

"Yes." He was sixty nine, and for most of the twenty-seven years he had worked as an editor for the university a dark cloud had hung over him as if he were kneeling under a guillotine operated by deans, department chairmen, and assorted administrators whom he had expected would sooner or later, like the Red Army soldiers, stop him and demand: *Document est?* He couldn't have provided proof of passing even first grade because according to the most important document of his life besides his marriage certificate, the document that had given him the citizenship of all refugees' desire, he was two years younger.

"I am aware that you are an angel appointed by God to free me."

"Don't be silly," she said. "I am only a fellow vestry member."

* * * * * *

The April sun reflecting off the American cars partly pulled up on the sidewalk of the narrow *Gretreidegasse* highlighted the imperfections of the yellow plaster on Mozart's House of Birth. Most of the cars belonged to the U.S. Army and were painted olive green. Salzburg was in the U.S. Zone of occupation. Only a few civilian cars, among them a new '49 Studebaker resembling the cockpit of a B-25 bomber, were parked close to the hotel Blane Gemz, a favorite with the American tourists. The Festspiel Haus was on the same side of the street. The pastry shops were open again with their wonderful confections made with sugar originating in the U.S. via the PX and the black market. There was also a smart clothing store selling Styer costumes, lederhosen, Tyrolean hats, and ski boots for prices few of the natives could afford and that were beyond the wildest dreams of the refugees from the Soviet Zone. To reach the American Zone and Salzburg the refugees had to crawl through and under barbed wire. Most of those who made it were men with past service in one of the fighting armies of World War II. Military experience was needed for survival because besides the barbed wire—stretched, woven, or laid down in nightmarish accordion pleats—this twentieth century evolutionary selection process also involved landmines and Red Army soldiers. It all worked against families in general, women and children in particular. They could not run as fast, crawl as far, or keep quiet as long as the unburdened single men could. Some families died together stepping on landmines, some were shot on the wires like bedazzled owls at sunup or died separately in work camps far from their homes or the place they so desperately tried to reach.

A tall, thin, black-haired young man with a leather Hungarian tank corps coat draped over his shoulder was peering through the shop window. The money he had in his pocket, representing all his financial worth, was the exact price of two hard rolls and a small glass of beer. It wasn't as if he coveted Tyrolean hats or Styer costumes. He didn't. When he was a boy, his mother had arrived home from one of the Salzburg Mozart festivals with a Styer costume and a green Tyrolean hat that had instantly transformed him into a figure of fun in his gymnasium class and soon transported him to a boarding school away from Budapest, his parents, his one and only friend Otto, and his dog Ricky, a gun-shy vizsla that wasn't good for anything other than being his dog. In spite of his father's considerable social standing, he was asked to leave the school, not only because he had beaten several of the boys with his riding crop, but because he had damaged school property when in his anger he overturned a lighted stove during Latin class.

The American tourists were also window shopping, loudly commenting on everything, the women as loud as the men. The main difference between him and them, besides his lack of citizenship and money, was his state of mind that vacillated between glorying in the April sunshine that affirmed his life and resenting it because his survival had turned him into a homeless stranger with no imaginable future in this world. He was hungry and too tired to want to go on. He was twenty-five years old.

With screeching tires a jeep halted for an instant then jumped the curb and stopped on the sidewalk blocking his way. He spun around, his combat knife thrust in front of him.

"Andre!" The driver was his friend, Otto, who had been in Salzburg for three months. He had a job delivering mail for some of the American agencies. "What's the matter with you?"

"It was the sound," he said. The NKVD had tried to drag him into their car when he was in Wien.

"You are in Salzburg now," Otto said. "You are in the US. Zone"

"I know." The Americans in their perfect movie-star clothing were looking at him. He stuck his knife into the top of his right boot.

"The MP's don't like knives. They will pick you up. You won't look good without papers."

"It wouldn't be so bad," he said. "They feed their prisoners thick slices of Spam, beets, green beans, and potato salad served on sectioned plates." Thick saliva in his mouth made him stop for a moment. "And as much bread as you want to eat. Remember Hans the Croatian? He was in for pandering."

"Get in. We'll have to get you some sort of a D.P card. Even in the US. Zone there's no safety for illegals. If the Soviets decide they want you back, the Americans won't do anything to help you. They have no idea what the communists are really like."

* * * * * *

He was lying on one of the *Lehen Kasserne's* lower bunks. The old military barracks on the banks of the river Salza were being used to house the people who had signed up for the International Relief Organization's European Voluntary Workers scheme that shipped stateless persons to countries requesting laborers. Awaiting Interpol check and the outcome of lung X-rays, the provisionally accepted were given food rations every other day. Each ration consisted of four small boxes of raisins, five dekagrams of red marmalade the consistency of soft cheese, and ten dekagrams of bread. He had eaten his first ration the moment it was handed to him, wanting to be filled to free his eyes from peering at the world through the narrow bore-hole of his stomach that squeezed every thought into a frozen compass arrow pointing at FOOD. After eating his ration he had lain down on his bunk remembering the summer he had made his first kite of reed and newsprint using flour paste for glue. It had a lovely octagonal shape that narrowed toward the long tail constructed of a discarded violin string and candy wrappers of different colors. He even painted the newspaper' skin a lovely blue, but the print showed through however much paint he used. Her maiden flight had made his heart race, partly from joy and partly from fear that the string would break. At one point when the kite was dancing over the Danube way up under the clouds he wanted to let go of the string thinking that it was too much for him to hold. But he didn't let go. He couldn't give up the blue kite to free himself for a glorious memory of the kite, illuminated by a golden sun, glissade into the clouds, a memory that could have stayed with him unsullied for as long as he lived.

After the first week, when it had become common knowledge that he had passed his lung X-ray, he had been offered packs of

144

cigarettes and bread as payment for standing in for a few men whose T.B., past or present, disqualified them from going anywhere. They didn't ask him for his help but further diminished his already tattered self-image by presenting him with a proposition as if he were a service provider like a prostitute who could not refuse a pack of cigarettes and a few Hershey bars. His mother would have dismissed them with a wave of her hand, muttering *epicier*, though not meaning grocers, but Philistines. Declining all payments, he was X-rayed fourteen times.

Interpol also passed him toward the end of the third week. It didn't matter that the D.P card that Otto had filched and altered with the aid of half an Irish potato made him two years younger.

The next day, Good Friday, he walked on the well-kept path leading toward the fort on top of *Monschberg*. He was thinking that he would never see Mirabel Garden's stone gnomes again. It was here that he sometimes snared pigeons. He always hated plucking the feathers that were beautiful-mostly electric-blue and soft-gray—even on the dead birds. He had cooked the birds over a trash fire when he had camped under one of the bridges with a view of Paracelsus' house. Looking down at the cathedral's greenish cupolas, the narrow coiling streets, the glinting Salza river, he felt Grace overflowing him and the town to obliterate the sins of recent memory: the massed flags with their swastikas and the manic shouting of hate whose end result was the screaming of children thrown into crematorium fires to add another chapter to the killing of the innocents. Only Grace or another Flood could wash away Sin that in its total, immediate reality had made the promised victory of good over evil incredible on Good Friday, Anno Domini 1949.

Three days later his group was taken by train to the Hook of Holland to be shipped to England.

"I'm two years older than what you see on my identification card, Father." Meg's father, his future father-in-law, was an Anglican priest. The congregations in Devonshire he served now in his retirement as a "guinea pig"—named thus because supply priests were paid one guinea for their services— actually addressed him as "Mister." They were sitting in the drawing room beside a marble fireplace filled with flowers. Through the open windows he could hear the gulls' cries punctuated by the rhythmic sound of shingle rolled by the sea.

"Surely that can be rectified." His almost father-in-law looked like the man in Country Gentlemen advertising Bentley automobiles and Scotch whiskey. He had first met him six months ago at London airport when he arrived home from Nigeria to begin his retirement. He and his wife, a South Carolinian, had been Anglican missionaries in Nigeria for the past twenty-five years. He had accompanied his father-in-law-to-be on the journey to The Croft, the family house in the village of Beer, overlooking the English Channel. On the long railway journey to Devonshire he confessed his sins, prefacing his confession with: *Quad vixi tege, quod vivam rege.* His father-in-law-to-be agreed to hide his past and guide his future life, again proving the efficacy of Latin, the dead language he had once hated.

"This isn't the time to complicate things by trying to explain about my papers. Joe McCarthy is making everybody paranoid."

Meg, with her dual citizenship, was already in hot water with the American Embassy because she had left the United States with her American passport but landed in the UK with her British one. Washington considered the use of her British passport an act of disloyalty. To keep her American citizenship,

146

the embassy said, she had to relinquish her British passport and promise to return to the U.S. in three months' time.

"Did you ever think of making a life for yourselves here in England?"

"We did." He wasn't another Heinrich Heine, who in his detestation of anything English wrote: *I might settle in England if it were not that I should find there two things, coal smoke and Englishmen; I cannot abide either.* He personally wouldn't have minded a little coal smoke in a moderately heated house, but if they stayed in the U.K., he would have remained indentured to the Ministry of Labour for five more years. He had served only two years of his allotted time in the European Voluntary Worker scheme. In America he would be free. Meg also wanted to go. She didn't consider either England or Nigeria "home." Most of the family on her mother's side lived on an island in the low country of South-Carolina. Her English father had been an only child.

The first time he had seen Meg was in Hartfordshire, at the Shenley Mental Hospital where the Ministry of Labour had sent him to be a kitchen porter. She was wheeling a stout bicycle by a herbaceous border of marigolds, lupines, delphiniums, and poppies that formed a proscenium lit by the sun that highlighted her short chestnut-colored hair. She was wearing a square-necked, black and white plaid summer dress with wide straps. Her face was beautiful in a well-bred English way. He was staring at her with the intensity of worshipers gazing at their icons hoping that through the visible focus they would glimpse the Invisible, hear the still small voice and understand the mystery of their own salvation. He was gazing at her because he had recognized her, his dream become flesh.

He must have been eleven or twelve when he had the dream. He was small for his age, but in the dream he was a tall man walking beside this girl. They were passing by a coffeehouse in

Budapest. His head was even with the overhead canvas that flapped now and again, the sound intermingling with the sound of spoons clinking on the sides of coffee cups and the barely perceptible susurration of newspaper pages turned on their bamboo frames. The small marble-topped coffee tables were set up on the gray asphalt sidewalk. Though they were not speaking there was an overwhelming sense of love between them that was different from the love he felt for his parents, his sister, his friend, Otto, or his imaginary dog, Chupy, who had never left his side when he was sick in bed. The street itself was paved with cobblestones that made the horses' hooves sound like Alberich's hammer. His Hungarian grandmother, sitting in a carriage, was waving her lorgnette at them. That was all there was to the dream but he never forgot it. Standing at the other side of the floral proscenium in his brown kitchen potter's coverall that in his mind created a deep chasm, a mile-wide orchestra pit between them, he had watched her wheel her bike toward a brick cottage that he always thought of as a *villa*, though he knew it housed the newly lobotomized patients under intensive retraining.

* * * * * *

Saint Peter's was a small pseudo-Norman church, built in the seventeen hundreds. Meg's father had been vicar here in Sommersal Herbert, Staffordshire, before going out to Nigeria. The sun shone through the clear, leaded windows onto the altar and the time-darkened furnishings. The wedding guests were outside with the photographer. Otto, his best man, waited for them in the doorway. He and Meg were standing in the back by the front under the choir stall and the organ pipes. On an ordinary pine table just below the bell pull lay their marriage certificate.

"You sign here, son." His father-in-law, wearing his cassock and surplice, was pointing at the place. In the box for the bridegroom's rank or profession, his father-in-law wrote in his strange southpaw-forced-to-use-his-right-hand-script: *Gentleman*, and in the box for the bridegroom's age: *Full*.

* * * * * *

"We'll need all the leaves," Meg said. They would have to stretch the oak dining room table to its limits. Everybody was coming. *Everybody* stood for the children and grandchildren. It was July the 8th. Their forty-fifth wedding anniversary.

The leaves for the dining room table were stored in the entranceway closet with the vacuum cleaner, raincoats, ponchos, winter gloves that they hardly ever used here in North Florida, pillows for the back porch that had been rained on and dried repeatedly, the threadbare tweed jacket that he wore on cold mornings in January and February to go down to the barn to feed the horses (his two good tweed jackets, ready for another revisit to England now that they were both retired, were stored in the guest room in a clothes bag filled with mothballs), flashlights, peculiar pop-up umbrellas that took to hiding at the first sound of rain, Meg's straw gardening hats, two wool scarves he had brought over from England and last wore in 1950 in Hartfordshire, one for going to bed, the other for going to work at the St. Albans Gas Works, an Irish tweed hat, the disguise he supposed would change his social status for the better, not realizing that in the 1950s St. Albans, being thought Irish was almost as bad as being Hungarian or Jamaican, bargain Christmas and birthday presents that would be forgotten if stored in the attic, and bags of beads for the children's dress-up wardrobe where Sarah, twenty months old, could not reach them.

149

Whenever he pushed back the closet's folding doors, he thought of The Croft, the village of Beer near Seaton, of the Devonshire countryside. Meg's parents were both dead and The Croft had been sold, turned into flats. When they went back for two years in '59 to be with Meg's parents, their children went to the village school, John into the infant class, and Sibet into second grade. The fishermen, whose children went to school with Sibet and John, had lived in the cottages in sight of the sea. They too were gone, the cottages refurbished and sold as weekend bungalows. They were total strangers now even at the Fishmonger & Fruiterers that used to be owned by Mr. Boalch, whose daughter was Sibet's best friend. The Fish & Chips shop that fried three days a week then went to Fridays only, had moved to Seaton. The news agent had died of cancer and his wife had moved to Exeter to be close to her children. Mrs. Hoskins, whose bakery shop he had visited three times a week because of the lovely smells and the Victorian Jubilee paraphernalia displayed on the counters and walls, had died too. Now only factory bread was available in Beer. The creamery had closed also, as had the butcher shop. Even Townsend Garage was closed.

Their friends, inherited from Meg's parents, were all gone. Mrs. Arnott was a sweet, curly headed, roly-poly little woman in her seventies who, on investigating a commotion issuing from her coal shed one stormy night, had found a Canada goose with a broken wing. She put a splint on the wing but when she removed it, the goose wouldn't even try to fly. Most afternoons, before he went down to the village school to collect the children, he watched Mrs. Arnott perched on a stool in her small garden flapping her arms while opposite her on a kitchen chair the goose was doing the same. Then Mrs. Arnott hopped down from her stool. It took several months of arm and wing flapping before the goose decided that it was safe to hop down. After a few more months the goose took to the air but always came back at night till one day a migrating flock called and Mrs. Arnott's goose joined them. A year later on another stormy night the goose returned to the coal shed for a two-day rest then left again for good. Mrs. Arnott had not named her goose because she believed that naming a wild thing like a pet was an indecent thing to do, yet when he had asked her if she ever wondered what had happened to her goose she burst out crying. Professor Olmstead was a retired Oxford classics don whose health could be gauged by his reading. "When I feel poorly I always read Hebrew. It's such a simple language," he would say, lying on a deck chair in his front garden, dressed in checkered tweed plus fours, weskit, jacket, and cap. And the Baroness Karg, known to most people as Mrs. Karg, the chambermaid at the Blue Dolphin, a royalist refugee from Austria whose childhood playmate had been the future kaiser and king of the Austro-Hungarian empire and whose dream—fulfilled at the age of seventy-six— was a room in the almshouse facing the playground of Beer's primary school where Sibet and John visited her on school days. Mrs. Spottswood, another unique character, whose pride in her dead husband's family could be overwhelming—one of the Spottswoods was the seventh governor of Virginia, and they were also connected to Mary Queen of Scots—was a kind, beautiful, generous lady who had indelibly established in his mind that sherry was a reward for going to church. She always served sherry after the services.

At the last visit they didn't know anybody and had no place to go home to. They would now be on par with the day trippers whose first order of business on arriving at Beer was the finding of the public conveniences located just below Jubilee by the blinking light that used to guide the fishermen home. There were small warnings signs stuck in the ground next to the bushes that flanked the pathways: Do not commit public nuisance.

Some primitive peoples performed an act of purification on the village square by burning the old, the worn out, the discredited, in the hope that they would be supplanted by something better. On the eve of the twenty-first century both he and Meg were ready for the pyre if the reality was the world as depicted by TV news, movies, miniseries, the arts, literature. Perhaps even as a young man he was peculiar. In '53 he had been the lone cowboy on a 1,200 acre ranch (a Brahman bull, fifty scrub-cows, two hundred steers, and three horses). He remembered one evening sitting next to two-year-old Sibet on the top step of their shack watching some cranes marching by on the St. Augustine pasture. Under a large pine tree a cow lay tiredly, her new calf standing on wobbly legs beside her. His happiness was a physical thing. He felt it in his chest, his throat, in his lips, which knew only one way to express themselves: to kiss this world of backaches and posthole diggers, barbed wire and cut hands, newborn calves and circling buzzards.

Once a month the owner's agent came to inspect the place and pay him his salary of ninety dollars out of which they had to furnish kerosene for their lamp and refrigerator. Other than the agent's monthly visit, the three of them were the only company for each other. Every Friday they drove to Sebring to buy supplies and watch people, but they always came back long before dark, long before the horses needed to be fed, even the week the Grand Prix races were held on the unused military airfield and the town was filled with strange, colorful people, many of them foreign. Time seemed safe and endless. Then his mother's letter came, but the stamps were not Hungarian. It had been posted from Austria. His sister had been killed. It was a political murder perpetrated by the communists. A few weeks later he was knocked down by a crazed steer. He lay next to the chute, hearing the half-choked blaring of frightened animals, the pounding of hooves, bodies pushed against planks, smelling the air filled with sweetish dust. He was penned just as he had penned the steers into the enclosure for the cattle trucks to haul away. Overhead the sky was a blue dome completely covering the earth.

* * * * * *

"Do you need any help with the leaves?" Meg called from the kitchen.

"No, thanks." Solicitude irritated him because it reminded him of his age. It also reminded him of his initial helplessness after the accident. He still missed the ranch. Everything he loved and his family needed was right there. Then it was over. Papers and birth certificates had become important once more and the Red Army soldiers' demand: *Document est?* again resounded in his head. He half expected to be stopped on the street by someone in uniform demanding to inspect his hands. People without calluses were the first to be selected for the labor camps.

"You needn't have brought all the leaves at once," Meg said.

"We'll need a tablecloth. One of the leaves isn't quite the same color."

"None of our tablecloths is big enough."

"We could use the new yellow sheet."

Once the sheet had been ironed to get rid of the fold marks it gave the table the solemnity of fair linen.

"What do you think?"

"It's lovely," Meg said. "We can use the blue napkins. Flowers, candlesticks, or both?"

"Both," he said, feeling tears welling up suddenly as if old age had robbed him not only of the control of his tears but even the

153

ability to predict their appearing. There had been both flowers and candlesticks on the altar of St. Andrew's for the Glory of God and in thankfulness for Otto's life. Forty-five years ago the solemnization of their matrimony could not have begun without Otto, the tier of his necktie, his best man, his guide, who had given him a persona in the U.S. Zone of Austria by the simple but bold expedient of cutting an Irish potato in half and using it as a rubber stamp. Otto had died two weeks ago.

* * * * * *

Nine-year-old Kate, his oldest grandchild, demonstrating gymnastics, was arching her body so that her feet touched the back of her head. The other children sat on the back porch steps watching her.

"John Gray do you want me to show you how to arch your back?"

"I'd rather do cartwheels." John Gray, six, hopped off into the grass and did a wobbly cartwheel. Sarah turned around, backed down the steps, then rolled in the grass. The dogs applauded with their tails.

He looked back through the glass door. The table with the pale yellow cloth, blue napkins, white china, flowers in a silver bowl flanked by tall ceramic candlesticks was festive. This was the same battered old oak table they had bought thirty years ago, paying five dollars a month for a year. It was strange how the most ordinary objects could be transformed into the numinous by the intent of the occasion. Even at the ranch when they were dirt poor Meg could transform their cypress planks and two sawhorses into a Christmas table with her flowers. She and the children had transformed him too—into a husband, father, and grandfather.

"Fadoux," Kate called, "Sarah is hungry." It was John Gray who had named him Fadoux for an unfathomable linguistic reason when he was two and a half years old.

"I want some-some," Sarah said.

"If you want some-some that's reason enough to go in."

John had already poured wine. Sarah was deposited in her highchair, ensconced in her plastic apron.

"The whole family is here, Fadoux," John Gray said.

Meg was looking at him from across the table. They were all looking at him, waiting for him to give thanks.

"For these and all Thy mercies," he began. He couldn't go on. He was overcome by stillness as if it were the moment before creation, before time and space, leaving him only the reality of God's hand reaching out to hold him upright.

An Eagle's Cry

It was five in the morning, the time in his experience—between four and five—when the condemned was wakened to be led out. It was always five in the morning that his stomach independently from his thoughts remembered another time, another country. He was only thinking of the lone, little goldfish he had put in the horses' drinking trough. His grandson had won it with a well-placed tennis ball at the Alachua County fair. There was no way he could tell the boy at the age of four that they should not bring it back home, that he only wanted to spare him the pain of seeing his little fish floating belly-up in a glass bowl. Trying to shield him from pain he proposed their horses' drinking trough as a home for Goldy. There was nothing else he could do. The fish had been named.

At the next morning's feeding, he had expected to see a dead fish floating on the surface of the water tank but other than bits of grass there was nothing. A month later when he was skimming the water with a bucket he had seen a much larger Goldy in the depths of the murky trough. The Extension publications on cattle and horse troughs he had been reading for years had been vindicated but it was a mixed blessing. He couldn't get Goldy out of his mind. Goldy alone in the tank. Goldy alone in his world unable to communicate. Goldy an inadvertent symbol. The blind had Braille, the deaf sign language but the Church that for centuries had taught illiterates through her stained-glass windows and symbols had lost the ability. Her vocal cords had atrophied from trying to speak in a falsetto to accommodate a people who, by and large, made their life decisions based on the state of their hormones or of the current fads. To make decisions based on 'Thus saith the Lord' was patronizingly assigned to the simple minded or was called "insultingly cruel" even by some Christian publications.

He lived among Western Christians whose most quoted theologians and bishops had created a 'robocop' theology that was part flesh, part politically correct, secular thought. They wanted Christianity without its revelation, without God the Father, Son, and Holy Spirit. Like King Nebuchadnezzar 's chief eunuch renaming Daniel, they wanted to rename the One beyond their ken to name. Their ideal of 'religion' was the Roman equitas that placed all religions on the same footing, but put beyond the pale certain of their brethren who believed with Origen of Alexandria as he had expressed it in the third century that the Christian religion has its origin in God's manifestation not in human sagacity, maintaining that salvation is possible only through Jesus Christ. That belief made them fail the politically correct Church's litmus test applied even to martyrs of the faith. Christians who were killed or put into concentration camps by the communists never passed the test either. They remained nameless, forgotten people.

In the United States, a country whose motto, "In God We Trust" was engraved on its currency, this same litmus test transformed the First Amendment of the Constitution into a censor if it became religion in the public square. It was like sitting at the foot of a Tower of Babel, trying to talk to his fellow Americans so that the blind would see and the deaf would hear. His worst nightmare was the fear that their ears and eyes were wide open.

He looked at the illuminated radio clock. It was six o'clock. He didn't want to turn on the light and wake up his wife. The pain he felt was overwhelming. He listened to it, trying to sort it out as he had tried in the war to sort out the sounds around him, believing that if he had classified them correctly he was safe provided it wasn't heavy artillery, mortars or B-29 bombers. But he could not classify this pain. There was no demarcation between the physical and the mental, no green line that would indicate one side or the other.

"Are you alright?" his wife asked.

"Yes." He touched her lovely, familiar body that over the years had kept his terrifying ghosts at bay. "Go back to sleep."

The dogs didn't want to leave the utility room. It was the first week in Advent and there was light frost in the air that turned the pastures a glittering white in the early morning light, regular north Florida November weather where later in the day the temperature would climb to the seventies. Most of the horses were outside the barn facing east towards the woods looking like people standing in the nave of a cathedral. With pricked ears they watched a small band of grazing deer. The deer had jumped over the fence from their San Felasco nature preserve.

In the total silence he could hear them crop grass then one of the horses stomped the ground and the deer froze into statues of speed and grace. They were all waiting, watching the white light expand as if seeing the moment of creation bringing forth a streak of green that no color chart had ever captured, then light pink deepening into rich purple, a royal robe edged with gold flung over it all. Then the birds began to sing, the deer were released and he knew with all certainty that a deaf Beethoven had heard what he had seen this morning in the first week of Advent and in his own joy rehearsed with the psalmist: 'Blessed is the man whom thou choosest, O Lord and causest to approach Thee.' Pain that seemed to have made a constant abode in him for the past few years had disappeared with the peculiar effect of a struck guitar string that would not resonate. He remembered the pain but its sting had gone as if to teach him that though there were no endings there were always beginnings that could come in the blinking of an eye, a trumpet blast or with the daily aesthetic glory of a sunrise.

The sky was blue now with white clouds like gossamer scarves flung in an ark against it. Samba the lightening-struck but surviving chestnut thoroughbred, who against all odds had reached Olympic level in dressage came up to nudge him in the back. He touched his nose then blew into his nostrils. The other horses came too, to have their noses touched. It was feeding time.

* * * * * *

At eight thirty he drove his grandson to preschool. Instead of driving straight back home he stopped at a small shopping center and parked in front of the *AQUARIUM CONNECTION*. The second he opened the door to the shop he was engulfed in the heat, smells and sounds of the pet store. There were large parrots gripping their perches with their claws that revolted him because they made him remember the retreat from the Ukraine where he had seen human hands turned into dark claws sticking out of the melting snow.

"What can I do for you, sir?" A young woman emerging from behind a large aquarium asked him.

"I'd like some goldfish. Nothing fancy. I need them for my horses' drinking trough."

"I didn't know people did that with goldfish."

"Oh yes. We already have one called Goldy. He's thriving."

"The little ones are four for a dollar."

"Yes, please."

"If you don't mind my asking. Where are you from? My major is linguistics." She was fishing in the tank with a tiny net.

"Alachua."

"That's not an Alachua accent," she laughed. "Before that."

"Hungary." Even to his own ears it sounded like a confession. He didn't want to be a hyphenated American.

* * * * * *

He put the fish in their water-filled plastic bag into the trough as he had been instructed. They needed to be acclimated for fifteen minutes before they were turned loose. He watched the little fish darting about in their prison as if trying to burst through the plastic walls, making it hard not to free them prematurely.

He looked up. An eagle was gliding with turned-up wing tips against the blue sky. It circled lazily, stopping at times, its wings stretched wide. Standing there at the water tank watching the four little fish darting about in their prison he wondered what an eagle was doing over the pasture. He had seen hawks before but not eagles.

Then the eagle cried with a loud voice and he knew that it was time. He took his pocketknife and slit the plastic prison walls setting the little fish free. Goldy, twice their size came to meet them.

Glory of All Lands

The acclivity of the pasture was hardly noticeable, yet when pulling the large bush-hog behind the tractor toward the five-board outer horse fence that separated their land from the San Felasco Nature Preserve, he had to stop to change down into second to keep the engine from laboring. The antique Ford 4000 couldn't be shifted on the fly. It was something that he was accustomed to just as he was used to living with the physical limitations of his own advanced years. What nobody had told him, nor had he found in his eclectic readings, was that alongside these age-imposed limitations there existed another phase of the human condition that illuminated a new sphere, a new environment, that revealed the true scale of things.

When jumping hurdles, the rider needs to align the horse properly all the way to that most difficult last fence to be able to clear it. The proper alignment between human beings is a necessity in keeping relationships going in spite of all the hurdles encountered in the course of a lifetime. Fifty-six years ago in 1946, when he had escaped from Hungary to Austria, then occupied by the four victorious powers (England, France, the Soviet Union and the United States), he had joined *Jeannette & Dodo*, a comedy dance routine, as the front legs of Dodo the zebra. At the sound of Glen Miller's "In the Mood," Jeannette entered first, in a black lace leotard covering her nude body and her red hair piled on top of her head. She always caused a near riot among soldiers of the four armies. Then Jeannette, imperiously waving a pink ostrich feather, she would call, "Dodo!" Dodo entered the night club floors or circus sawdust rings (Medrano's or Reberning's) attempting to prance like one of the Lipizzaners at their famous Viennese show place. Slightly inebriated to overcome stage fright, he always felt himself transformed into both horse and rider, and ignored his partner's plea (Dodo's hind legs had to walk bent over) to slow down. The only time he felt safe from the Soviets was inside Dodo's papier-mâché head and canvas body. The NKVD were picking up political refugees from the streets and hotels of Vienna. He had known some of the vanished people. Two of them had stayed in the room next to his at the Hotel Wandl, where the management accepted people without passports. Years later the two vanished men had resurfaced. He found their names in Aleksandr Solzhenitsyn's *Gulag Archipelago*.

Vienna's international zone was policed by the MP's of the four occupying powers riding together in a Jeep with one of them in charge for three months. The day before the Soviets' rotation was coming up he walked to the Radetzky barracks where the French Foreign Legion was billeted and signed up. The next day he was on a train with the other recruits traveling through the different sectors toward an unknown destination. The Foreign

164

Legion took all his personal papers then gave him a new identity. After three months, when their initial training had ended and they had received their white hats, the noncommissioned instructors and his comrades began to call him *feu d'artifice*, a pop-off with the unstable temper of a firecracker that had created a safe no-friendship zone around him. He had not always rejected friendship. Arriving with the Hungarian Army in the Ukraine on the Eastern Front in '43, he had made many friends among the Hungarian and German soldiers, and even some of the Ukrainian civilians living in Kiev. Before the general retreat the fighting in the Ukraine consisted of advance, retreat, and advance again. After the last advance into Kiev he visited the district where his civilian friends had lived. He had found them murdered. The bodies were still warm. The beautiful oldest daughter's name was Irena. By the time he joined the Foreign Legion in '47, he believed that friendship with him caused people to die. He knew his thinking was illogical, still he could not take the chance.

In the distance on the pasture closest to San Felasco Nature Preserve a flock of wild turkeys, looking like a group of dark-caped French police marching purposefully against demonstrators, spooked the large four-year-old warm-blood mares grazing there. The one called Nonie, named after his son John's beloved Sunday school teacher of forty years ago, had the build, bloodline and intelligence to become an international show jumper. Unfortunately, breeding and training horses wasn't an exact science. There were many reasons why this might not come about.

He turned the tractor around, stopped, shifted up into third and let out the clutch, rolling easily toward the back fence and the woods. Deer were slowly moving behind a screen of pine trees.

There had not been any sound of gun shots since about four months ago when John started negotiating to buy the eighty acres of land adjacent to their own twenty-five acres. The owner had allowed the hunting of the semi-tame deer in exchange for the hunter cutting a fire-lane twice a year. The fire-lane cutter had then invited his friends to set up their own deer-stands. Shooting the deer that hopped over the fence from San Felasco Nature Preserve was as easy as shooting grazing cattle. It was not hunting. Recently, John had dismantled five of the deer stands even though negotiations for the land were still going on. John had asked him to help but he didn't want to cross over barbed wire. He did not want to dream about land that may never be theirs.

Before turning again he stopped the tractor. There was the albino stag with the herd watching him from behind a barbed wire fence stretched outside their own five- board horse fence at the edge of the woods. It wasn't the first time that the white stag had looked at him generating memories of the boy who was told over and over again of the legend of the Magical Stag that led the two brothers, Ugor and Magor to the Carpathian basin. Perhaps he, himself had now met his own magical White Stag who was trying to entice him to enter the woods beyond the barbed wire. He remembered standing with his grandfather more than sixty years ago on their side of another barbed wire fence several thousand miles from here, looking across to what had been his family's land for generations before the peace treaty of Trianon had been signed two years after the conclusion of World War I. The Pact took its name from a palace in Versailles, the scene of the peace conference where Hungary lost two-thirds of its pre-war territory. This knowledge of the loss of his country, that included part of his own family's settlement, he had carried in him like a piece of shrapnel. Trianon remained a painful reality

166

even though he had become a declared American with no hyphenations in 1954.

His love for the United States had started in earnest when he had first heard Sputnik's signal in 1957 and realized that his awe-inspiring new country had become vulnerable just as his own little five-foot-two mother living under the communist regime in Budapest had become vulnerable as a class-enemy that made her eligible for deportation to the Hungarian countryside to die in the winter in an unheated barn. After September 11, 2001, he had realized that dying at the hands of terrorists now would be as nothing for the fifty-two years of his life lived here and for the privilege of saying: *Civis Americanus sum* as proudly as a veteran of the Roman legions would announce his citizenship. Curiously though, admitting these feelings to some of his intellectual friends would have been more difficult than confessing to an illicit love affair.

All the horses were facing the woods, their ears erect as if they too were waiting for a signal. Then the White Stag turned his head and with one bound disappeared from sight as if someone had pushed the *off* button on the remote. The rest of the herd flowed after him with the undulating motion of dolphins, leaving behind only the sound of their passing.

He was born in 1923, three years after the Peace Treaty of Trianon had sliced off two-thirds of the land that had been Hungary for a thousand years leaving behind an ungainly shape resembling the armless and legless veterans left on street corners in Budapest propped up in wicker-baskets that had wheels like baby carriages, their trunks dressed in army tunics, their caps on the pavement next to them, silently begging. He was not quite eleven when he started at the Piarist Gymnasium where Fr. Szilard made sure that they would never forget their first geography lesson. Fr. Szilard was a tall, thin man, intimidating in his black cassock and white hair. He had stood with eyes closed in front of a rolled up map attached to the blackboard, reciting the acolyte's responses from the Holy Mass that most of the boys knew by heart:

"*Quia tu es, Deus, fortitudo mea, quare me repulisti? Et quare tristis incedo, dum*
   affligit me inimicus?"

For Thou art God, my strength; why hast Thou cast me off? And why do I go sorrowful, whilst the enemy afflicteth me?

There was a short pause then Fr. Szilard opened his gray, sorrowful eyes to reach up to pull a string to unfurl a map of Hungary showing the thousand-year-old border outlined in red like the Holy Days in the missal. The remaining one-third in the middle of the map was surrounded by the crown of thorns.

He didn't know when he had first heard the word: "Trianon." The word always seemed to be there like a dark shadow that could materialize even in the midst of games played in the schoolyard forcing them to be quiet as if visiting the sick and dying. The fact of the mutilation of their land was always before him. The ungainly shape framed with the crown of thorns was depicted everywhere on small, square, flat metal plaques nailed to front doors. It was nailed to their own front doors both in the country and the city forcing him to remember Trianon every time he went in or out. Most of the people he knew were irredentists who without consciously thinking about it were preparing their souls to accept any bargain with the Devil in exchange for the return of their land. They wanted the crown of thorns surrounding the ungainly shape to be gone.

In June all his immediate family were at home at their truncated settlement whose name they carried with slight spelling variations for centuries. On the land remaining in their possession they grew wheat, corn, potatoes and some truck crops mostly for the settlement's own use. The twenty-five acre grape and apricot orchards, plum and cherry trees provided their ordinary drinking-wine, snaps and plum-brandy.

The main business of the settlement was horses: light workhorses, remounts for the cavalry, carriage horses, sporting horses, polo ponies and racehorses. Before Trianon the horses were bred and trained on pastures that now had become 'the other side'. He had been told many times by his family, servants, and the sharecroppers that on the night of June 3rd, 1920, all their horses were ridden or driven over across the newly created border (the colts and fillies up to two weeks old were hobbled and laid in carts, their mares trotting beside them) before the barbed-wire fences went up on the fourth. His grandfather and father were on the drive as were his grandmother and mother riding sidesaddle. Most of the sharecroppers of Cuman ancestry, regardless of where their own five, ten, fifteen or twenty acres fell on this new divide, elected to leave with the horses.

Their ancestors had ridden with his own ancestors from Asia seeking refuge in Hungary in the 13th century. Two hundred years later, when they had become absorbed into the native population, they were still fighting and dying for the land that was granted to them in the first place to keep them fighting and dying for the kings of Hungary. The Cuman chiefs, Uzur and Tolon, were members of the Great Council of Teteny, which settled the provision of the law of 1279 regarding Cuman settlements, their own settlement among them. The only dissimilarity remaining between the Cuman descendants and their Hungarian hosts, beside some slight physical differences, were the color combinations used by the Cumans in decorating carts, carriages, harnesses, pottery and some of the clothing made at the settlement.

Every year, on June 3rd, his grandfather and father held a ritual commemorating the ride across the imposed border. When he was eight, big enough to canter one of their retired polo ponies, he was allowed to participate. He was awakened by his father just before daylight to have breakfast with his grandfather, his grandfather's driver whom he had been taught to address as Uncle Szekeres, and his father. They gathered in the huge kitchen, sitting around the large, much-scrubbed pine table. The stove was not lit on the mornings of June 3rd. Because nobody had ever explained the reason for it, the cold stove had become for him an introit for their day of remembrance.

In front of his grandfather sitting at the head of the table was a chopping block made from the squared-off bottom of an oak barrel. On it lay a thick, wide strip of cured bacon rubbed with paprika and a large, round loaf of bread. Beside the chopping block a carafe filled with water-like liquid smelled strongly like the still set up in the woods far from their house. There was nothing intimidating about his grandfather, this descendant of Kuthan who had led fifty-thousand Cumans from the mouth of the Volga to Hungary in a headlong, horse-killing flight from the conquering Mongols. His grandfather had none of the fierceness of the ancestors yet when he made a request of any inhabitant of the settlement, his wish would become an instant *irade:* unbreakable, permanent, revered like a national parliamentary decree.

Grandfather cut chunks of bread and bacon and passed them around, then poured plum brandy into small, dented silver goblets. After handing them around he lifted his arms saying: "He who gave us food to eat, His Name be blessed."

"Amen," they said and opening their pocket knives began to cut pieces of bread and bacon.

"Isn't Mr. Bonyak coming?'

"He was needed at the birthing barn," his father said. "Get yourself some milk, Andre."

Milk tasted horrible with bacon and bread. This bacon had been rubbed both with paprika and garlic. His grandfather believed garlic was a remedy of great efficacy.

Uncle Szekeres was standing at the head of a matched pair of gray Shagya geldings, Sultan and Pasha. The breed, developed mostly from desert Arabians, was named after a potent stallion whose progeny dominated the pedigree. His grandfather could recite the lineage a long way back with its occasional infusion of thoroughbreds and Lipizzaners. The original Arab stallions brought to stud were crossed on local Arabian mares and mares with a lot of Arabian blood, very much the process, his father had told them, that developed the thoroughbred in England. He had learned a lot listening to the grownups discuss the history of the Hungarian Nonius, Gidran, Furioso-North Star and even the English thoroughbreds, though only his parents could read the English studbooks. As a girl in France his mother was taught by an English nanny. In Hungary she spoke English with a 'companion', a refugee who had been once a lady-in-waiting at the court of Czar Nicholas II. His father had studied in England before World War I and brought back some of their horse-breeding ideas. When driving he always started the horses with an English word that sounded like *wah-kon*. Slapping the horses with the reins to start them moving was bad form even if his grandparents' driver Mr. Weber, who drove the closed carriages when they were in Budapest, always did so.

Uncle Szekeres wore a white shirt buttoned up to the neck, a black livery hat with a black ribbon hanging down the back and black britches inside black boots. Sultan and Pasha were hitched to an open four-seat runabout painted black then lacquered and decorated with pencil-thin red lines around the fenders. Because of the springs the carriage was high off the ground. There was a step made of wrought-iron attached to the underside between the seats. It looked like a flattened-out ladle. The front wheels were smaller than the back ones. The hubs on the front wheels were used as steps to get up to the front seat. Hanging from the back of the equipage was a large canvas envelope that held two folding card-tables, five folding chairs, an eight-millimeter Mannlicher rifle and a sixteen-gauge shotgun. On the floor between the seats was a large willow picnic basket.

His mother, dressed in a dirndl, came out of the house walking between his grandfather and father. Grandfather was dressed like Uncle Szekeres but for his green Tyrolean hat.

"*A bientot*," his mother said, waving farewell. It always embarrassed the boy when she lapsed into French.

"God be with you," Grandfather called.

His father drove from the right-hand side of the seat. Grandfather sat beside him. Uncle Szekeres was the last to get into the carriage. The boy watched the horses ears tilt backwards waiting for *wah-kon*, then when his father said it, the ears pointed forward and they were off. The carriage swayed then steadied when Pasha and Sultan began to trot, their hooves striking the dirt road sounding solemnly like the muffled drums at military funerals. The sun was rising a pale gold, the color of his sister's heart-shaped locket with the picture of Jesus in it. He wanted time to stop where he would always be in the company of his father, grandfather, Uncle Szekeres, Sultan and Pasha on a mission of utmost importance. He had become conscious of his own soul a week ago when he was told that ponies had no souls. He had been praying for Szello, his white pony, who had developed skin cancer on his backside. Now his soul was swelling inside his chest like a birthday balloon that was too close to the candles and might burst at any moment. He felt Uncle Szekeres's hand on his head like a blessing. It made not crying very difficult.

"When you are fourteen I'll teach you to drive a four-in-hand," Uncle Szekeres said.

Fifteen miles from their house, that the people of the settlement called 'headquarters', they stopped by a well surrounded by three courses of logs. Beside it a tall contraption resembling an asymmetric capital A was used to draw water into the wooden trough. After the horses were watered they pulled the carriage into the shade of a large mulberry tree where the horses were unhitched. The boy hung nosebags on them then he and Uncle Szekeres set up the folding tables close together, and covered them with a checkered tablecloth. His father brought over the picnic basket and placed a bottle of wine on each of the four corners of the table and three other bottles in the middle of the table. There was a light breeze that moved the grass and some of the trees in the distance.

"Shall I bring the Mannlicher, Father?"

"No need," his father said. He was looking toward the invisible border beyond the woods. "I can almost smell the acacia trees."

"Mr. Bonyak said that in 1920 you left all the houses and barns standing when you should have burned everything down." The boy was setting up a tripod for the cast-iron cauldron for Uncle Szekeres' fish soup with paprika. "He said that you and grandfather even left Meeshee Kemenche behind in your great rush. "

"His name is Mihaly Kemenche, Andre. You address him as *Mister* Kemenche. It was his choice to stay behind to help with the birthing of some of his own mares. We left all the buildings intact because we expected to be going back in a few months."

"In the twelfth century," Grandfather said, "Bonyak's great-great-great grandfather was a famous fighting chieftain. The Russians didn't like him and called him Bonyak the Mangy. Sadly that's how he's remembered today. When you skip rope you children never sing about his valor, only about Bonyak the Mangy. Am I right?"

"Yes, Grandfather."

"Poor Bonyak, it still upsets him. That's why he gets drunk once a month and breaks up the bowling alley," Uncle Szekeres said, pouring the makings of the fish soup into the cauldron.

"I would like to go over and see our land, Father. I know how to be invisible."

"No," his father said. "This isn't about playing cowboys and Indians."

"Or being invisible," Grandfather said. "It's about saving you from heartbreak. I long to see the stream that I played in and so do your father and Szekeres. It breaks our hearts that we can't watch you swim in it or smell the acacia woods and hear the bees collecting for their hives. You don't really miss land that you don't know, have no memories of. We might never go back in my lifetime. We want to save you from a heartbreak. "Grandfather pulled out his watch and looked at it with great deliberation. "It's about time."

Just as he said that a figure materialized. One minute there were only the trees, bushes, and the tall grass interspersed with clusters of nettles, in the next minute one of the clumps revealed a bandy-legged small man with graying-black hair and tanned skin stretched over high cheekbones. He was carrying a croker sack.

"Meeshee," Grandfather said, lifting his arms. The boy had seen photos where his father looked like the Eiffel Tower standing next to Mr. Kemenche. They were both wearing their World War

174

I uniforms with the big silver medal prominently displayed on their chests. The boy always heard 'Meeshee' mentioned on his father's birthday. They were both born in the same year on April Fools' Day. There were often photos too, of Mr. Kemenche in his jockey colors in the winner's circle with Grandfather. Mr. Kemenche was their winningest steeplechase jockey before the War.

Mr. Kemenche was standing in front of Grandfather trying to kiss his hand. Grandfather was holding him like a big bear saying: "Meeshee, Meeshee," as if he were trying to memorize a foreign name.

When the fish soup was ready, Uncle Szekeres lifted the cauldron onto the table next to a stack of soup bowls, and the big round loaf of bread and the large jar of honey that Mr. Kemenche had brought from the other side in his croker sack. Grandfather sat at the head of the table. Just to the right of him covered in khaki canvas was a large canteen. The boy knew that it contained their best plum brandy for after dinner when the real talking started. His grandfather told him once when they were quail hunting that drinking plum brandy always made him and the company more pleasant. It also dissolved his kidney stones.

"He who gave us food to eat," Grandfather prayed, "His name be blessed."

"Amen," they said.

"Meeshee," Grandfather said, "cut three slices of your bread, please."

Mr. Kemenche took the long knife, made the sign of the cross on the underside of the bread, then cut three slices and gave them to Grandfather. Grandfather broke them in half, handed each of them a piece, kept one for himself, then laid the remaining half to the right of him for a stranger who might come to their table.

"Andre, you pass out the soup bowls," Grandfather said.

175

While his father was pouring wine he passed around the filled-up bowls. Then he was lifting his glass like the men to drink a silent toast and sprinkle some of the wine on the ground. The fish soup was hot and had a lovely color from the paprika. He carefully broke off pieces from his slice of bread to eat with the soup. One did not tear into the staff of life like a wild beast his father had told him.

When the men were finished eating he collected the soup bowls and the spoons and took them to the well to wash them. He listened to Mr. Kemenche talking about the "other side": the names of the people who had died since last year, the number of babies who had been born, the people who had married, the families whose sons had been sent away for fighting while drunk and disorderly or simply because they were Hungarians. Then Grandfather, Father and Uncle Szekeres told their stories that included the horses too. When he sat down at the table, Mr. Kemenche asked him what he wanted to do when he was grown up. He would join the hussar regiment they had all served in, he told him, and after he had made captain he would come home like his father and grandfather to work with the horses. And ride in the steeplechase like Mr. Kemenche.

The men clapped their hands, then Grandfather poured plum brandy into the dented silver goblets then reached for the visitor's bread and broke off a piece for each of them to steep in their drink.

"Next year will see justice for Hungary and I won't need to skulk around anymore," Mr. Kemenche said. "I'll take you with me Andre to see the rest of your home."

He shifted down again for another pass up toward the road. Though they had a drought in March and April, the Bahia grass was tall and tasseled, rich enough that they had to restrict the ponies to night grazing only. The ponies, unlike most of the large horse breeds, were thrifty animals who could easily founder on the rich grass. A flock of cattle egrets landed on the pasture to follow the tractor like bow waves. They were picking up the fleeing grasshoppers.

John-Gray, his tall, thin thirteen-year-old grandson, was hailing him from the road. He drove up to the fence, shut off the engine and took off his earmuffs. The neighbor's donkey three miles away was braying.

"What's up, John-Gray?"

"Dad told me to give you a hand with the rest of the hay bales. He doesn't want you climbing around in the hayloft."

"Is your dad at home?"

"No, he went to town to see the lawyers. Do you think we'll get it, Grandfather. Do you think we'll get the land?"

"I don't know. We'll just have to be patient. You go on up to the barn. I'll come and help you as soon as I've finished mowing." He put the earmuffs back on, cranked up the engine and turned around for another pass toward the pinewood.

He was thirteen, the same age as his grandson, the last time he had taken part in the June 3rd commemoration ride. The sky was aquamarine that day dotted with white clouds that looked like the big pillows on the sharecroppers painted beds with their carved bedsteads. The beds were in the "clean rooms" that nobody ever slept in. His father was again driving Sultan and Pasha with Grandfather sitting beside him. He, himself, sat on the back seat between Uncle Szekeres and Mr. Bonyak, who told them he had heard a prediction on Radio Budapest last night about the recovery of the lost lands in the near future.

"One of our Free Corps groups already got into a firefight with their border guards."

"Once a thing like this gets started," Uncle Szekeres said, "there is no way to stop it. Close to the border we can expect to be shot at. We should have left Andre at home"

"I've known how to use a gun since I was seven," the boy said.

"I wouldn't mind shooting at them myself," Mr. Bonyak said. "Do we want our land back or do we just sit on our arses?"

The logs around the well had lost their bark but otherwise nothing had changed from the year before. The horses were unhitched in the shade of the mulberry tree. He hung on their nosebags then went to collect dry wood. Mr. Bonyak set up the tripod for the cauldron. While waiting they talked about Mr. Kemenche who had given up on reuniting with his Hungarian fiancee and had married a widow woman with two children who lived on the other side and wasn't even a Hungarian. Grandfather, who was a great self-taught historian, told them that *Kemenche* meant 'little bow' in the Cuman language.

"As in a bow and arrow, Grandfather?"

"Yes, Andre. One of Kemenche's ancestors must have been very good with his bow and arrow. He and another Cuman chieftain by the name of Tort-oyul—that means 'five sons'— killed king Ladislas IV."

"Mr. Kemenche never told me he had a hero for an ancestor like we have in Kuthan."

"Murderers are never heroes, Andre. Remember the story I told you about the four knights who murdered Saint Thomas Becket?"

"Yes, Grandfather."

"Do you think that the descendants of those knights would brag about their murderous ancestors? Not that Ladislas IV was any saint."

178

As they got closer to the appointed time all talking ceased. He watched his father go to the canvas envelope hanging from the back of the carriage and lift out his rifle. It was the same sporterized military Mannlicher with which he hunted wild boar and deer. The way his father listened with his whole body reminded him of Zsandar, his own Hungarian sheepdog, who was afraid of storms. Zsandar always knew when a storm was on its way even though he, himself couldn't hear or smell it coming. It was the same now watching his father motioning to Mr. Bonyak to get the shotgun loaded with buckshot.

Without warning one of the wine bottles on the corner of the table shattered, then he heard a succession of gunshots and a terrible sound like the magnified death scream of a rabbit. The aquamarine sky whirled. He saw grass and the nettles with their white flowers telling everybody to keep away. His grandfather and Uncle Szekeres were covering him with their bodies hustling him toward the logs surrounding the well.

"Your father and Bonyak will take care of it." Grandfather was breathing heavily. "You don't need to be afraid."

Looking over the logs he saw his father crouching close to the ground signaling Mr. Bonyak with his left hand. They looked like large bugs communicating with their antennae before they began scuttling toward the woods. There were more shots. He was praying, offering a bribe, an exchange of himself for the life of his father.

Lying in safety behind the logs surrounding the well he felt that his love for his father had become a terrible crushing weight that preempted everything else in his life and made even ordinary breathing a chore beyond his strength.

He heard Mr. Bonyak's shotgun and got up to peer over the logs again. Something was thrashing about in the woods. The Mannlicher fired: *one . . . and a two . . . and a three* in measured dancing school rhythm: *one chasse' . . . two chasse' . . . turn*. The shotgun boomed again. The thrashing ceased. The silence lasted and lasted making his muscles cramp. Then there was a single shot. It was the Mannlicher.

His father emerged from the woods carrying his rifle under his right arm like a hunter. His face was white. The wound from the War showing in his open-necked shirt was a pulsating red slash.

"Let's pack up." Father said. "We move out."

"Meeshee," Grandfather began.

"He is dead. They got to him first."

"Why for God's sake?"

"I don't know."

"We must take him home," Grandfather said. "Bonyak, cut the barbed wire so we can get him out."

"No, Father. His widow needs him more than we do."

"Of course," Grandfather sighed. "You are right."

"Who are they?" Uncle Szekeres wanted to know.

"I don't know." Father said. "Now they are three dead men in green coveralls."

"They had two French rifles," Mr. Bonyak said. "and a Russian long barrel sniper rifle." He was reloading the shotgun.

"Andre, you go and calm down the horses," Grandfather said. He reached for the plum brandy in the canteen and took a long pull. He was crying.

* * * * * *

John-Gray pitched down the last bale on top of those already stacked. From the cracks between the floorboards of the loft, dust and sediment was settling down slowly on the cement breeze way.

180

"One of the twin fawns is grazing in the aisle, Grandfather. Nonie is looking at her over the fence."

"What did you think about Nonie and Nicky coming in one-two ? Nonie got an eighty nine."

"Mom told us that one of the judges wanted to buy her." What do you think, Grandfather?" John-Gray was climbing down the ladder. "I'd miss her a lot."

"Me too."

"I'm going back to the house now, Grandfather. Mom doesn't like Sarah to be at home by herself. Did I tell you I'm building a megalopolis on the computer?"

He watched John-Gray talking to the horses as he cut through pastures, opening and closing gates. Sitting on one of the canvas chairs they kept down at the barn he remembered how as a boy he thought that his soul was like a birthday balloon that could pop at any time. Hearing the dogs welcome John-Gray as he entered the woods between their houses he realized that nothing had changed. What birthday candles could do to balloons, love could do to his soul.

* * * * * *

He was fifteen, at home from school on a September afternoon when Grandfather said that he was tired, walked down to the barn and lay down in an empty stall. It was the hounds howling that brought them down to see what was wrong.

"This is only the husk now, Andre," his father said. "Grandfather is out of harm's way. He is home safe."

He was seventeen when his father died on April Fool's Day, his forty-sixth birthday. A piece of shrapnel lodged in his body since the 1917 fighting on the Eastern Front had migrated toward his heart and suddenly killed him. The day after his father's death he woke up to a lovely spring morning, alive with light and sound and bird song. The breeze coming through the open window brought in clean spring smells and made the curtains dance. Then with unbearable intensity, the first shock returned. His father was dead. He wanted the world to be dark, draped with a black cloth forever. His father was dead.

He got up, washed, brushed his teeth then went to 'their' room. His mother turned her face toward him and said: "We are not a family anymore, Andre. We are not a family anymore."

At barely twenty he ended up on the Eastern Front in the latest *Toten Tanz*, in the never ending conga line stretching back to Kuthan, Tolon Uzur , to dance behind his own grandfather, his father, Uncle Szekeres, Mr. Kemenche, Mr. Bonyak and all the other men of his tribe. Because they had taught him their history, he knew that he was not in any worse peril than they had been and that this war would not end all wars either. He was only one in a long line of men living with horses and other riders who by some historical accident was placed at a certain geographical location to kill or be killed. He was what the Germans called an *Aufklaerer*, the eyes and ears of the Army serving in a reconnaissance unit. An old family legend told about a taltos ancestor, the shaman Ituk—'dog head'—the complimentary name given him for his second sight and the instinct that allowed him to sniff out the enemy hiding in ambush. His own clairvoyance—they had lost neither man nor beast since his arrival at the unit—had given him a special status. Much older men—men in their late twenties and even in their thirties—would speak to him about their premonitions that made him think that the past and present had converged in his person to single him out even among the uniformed sameness of soldiers.

Six months later his life had changed. The horses were dying—warmbloods couldn't take the harsh Russian winters—and the unit was disbanded. He ended up in an armored division where reading the mechanical manuals was akin to reading in a literature class an acrostic poem where the first letter of each line spelled out a hidden message that to him alone remained concealed to the amusement of his teachers and classmates. On the endless white steppes of Russia he needed alcohol to suppress his rising hysteria caused by the sensation that he had become a blind idiot blundering around, while the unseen enemy was shooting at him and the people he was supposed to lead.

The final chapter came less than a year later when the Red Army reached the family settlement, his home in Hungary, raped the women they could find, and drove off all the horses. For good measure they pulled down all the shelves in his family's library to build a campfire in middle of the parquet floor and smashed the venerable Ming vase that was part of the trousseau his mother brought from France. In another three months the remainder of the land was confiscated and he had become an escaped prisoner.

* * * * * *

Sitting on his canvas chair under the fan in the breeze way now that the sediment and dust from the hayloft had settled on the cement floor, he was looking toward the pine trees bordering the woods beyond their own five-plank horse fence. Though it was not visible, he was conscious of the barbed wire that separated their land from the woods and the eighty-acre parcel his son was negotiating to buy. From where he was sitting he could see the horses' round training pen and the wild turkeys perching on the top planks. The ones on the shady side looked like dark weather-stained gargoyles. The others, spotlighted by the sun's theatrical illumination, had become unreal greenish-gray metalized beasts, characters in a fantasy picture. He had nothing left to do at the barn yet he was reluctant to leave waiting for something vaguely perceived, something outside the periphery of his sight that with the turning of his head could disappear like the albino stag in a flash of white, perhaps never to be seen again.

Like their horses and dogs he too recognized the sound of the family cars and trucks. He got up just as his son drove into the front paddock. The back door of the car flew open and John-Gray scrambled out.

"We got it, Fadoux!" he shouted, reverting to the childhood name he had given his grandfather when he was two. "We got it."

His son was out of the car too. "Daddy, I just signed the papers!" Because of the slant of the land his son looked even taller. "We won't have to climb over the barbed wire anymore," he said waving a small bottle of bourbon above his head. "It's ours!"

The three of them were standing in front of the barbed wire fence. The pine trees towering at the edge of the dark woods had grown over the barbed wire like overlarge fence posts, stretching the wires drum tight. Just behind the wire where the sun could reach unhindered, black-eyed Susan stood three deep like a curbside homecoming crowd, their funny yellow hats with the brown discs on top undulating in the slight breeze.

"Well let's cut the barbed wire," John said. "You make the first cut Daddy."

His son once told him that anything put into a computer could not really be lost, that the text would remain in the hard-drive's memory ready to surface at the touch of the right combinations of keys. Now the touch of the taut top wire triggered his own memories warning him to get down fast before somebody opened up with a machine gun.

"Here's the fencing tool, Grandfather."

He fought the urge to get down on his stomach, and start cutting from the ground up. That's how he would have done it in the war. The top wire parted with the sound of a snapped guitar string, then the second and the third, each a halftone lower on the musical scale. "You cut the rest, John-Gray. Don't stand too close." He watched his grandson snipping the remaining two strands thinking that because the boy had never heard the sound of a gun fired in hate he would remember this moment only as a happy ribbon-cutting ceremony.

He followed them through to the other side out of the harsh sun to stand among the soaring trees feeling as if he had stepped inside a dim, cool cathedral dominated by the Real Presence. There was goldenrod stretching up from the ground like many-branched candelabra and tall purple blazing star on a square stage lit by the sun coming through an interruption in the canopy. John-Gray was ranging ahead of them like a bird-dog.

"Beetles got most of the young pines," John said. "We'll have to cut and burn the whole lot of them to stop the infestation. The lower part we can turn into pastures. At the highest point I want to build a screened-in tree house with no electricity. "

It was quite a steep climb. They were walking past fiddlehead cinnamon ferns. There was bracken at the edge of the woods, some of it rust colored.

"You alright Daddy? Not much further."

Then they were at the highest point with a few large hardwood trees and climbing yellow jessamine forming a half-circle. They could see down into San Felasco Nature Preserve. A tribe of wild turkeys, a circle of black dots from this distance, sat around a large shady tree. Deer grazed at the edge of one of the lakes.

"My God," he said lifting his arms. For some reason he was thinking of his mother's smashed Ming vase only now it was

185

glued together, the missing parts patched with clay like an archeologist's reconstruction, the lovely shape perfectly formed again.

"Let's sing the doxology," John-Gray said.

They sang together: "Praise God from whom all blessings flow . . .," then John unscrewed the bourbon bottle and passed it to him. He lifted the bottle toward the heavens then took a big swig. He sprinkled a few drops of bourbon on the leafy soil and passed the bottle to his son. John drank, and sprinkled the soil.

"Stick your tongue in the bottle, John-Gray so you can taste it."

"I don't like the taste of it, Dad." John-Gray generously sprinkled the base of a tree.

"That's enough, John-Gray," he said, taking the bottle away. "Too much bourbon's not good for trees."

Why he was alive when others had died he didn't know. He knew only that he was not a passive, inert product of the universe, a chemical formula that could be replicated endlessly with small variations in color and size. That he was here on this land his son had purchased was a sign to him of the presence of God and not a blind happenstance.

"Did I ever tell you about Uncle Szekeres?"

"Yes, Daddy."

"Szekeres' means "carter" in English," John-Gray said. "My great-great-grandfather found a brand new baby laid in a cart. He took him home and named him 'Szekeres'."

"After the first frost gets rid of the mosquitoes and chiggers we'll camp up here and tell stories," John said.

"Sarah's favorite is the story about Meeshee Kemenche riding a Gidran/Thoroughbred-cross in the Grand National and in the middle of it they are turned into a Centaur to win the race," John-Gray said. "She told me that when she jumped for the first time over a two-foot hurdle she and Ring-around-the-Rosie turned into a Centaur."

"For a nine year old your sister is one great and imaginative rider."

"It's time to leave," John said. "We've got things to do at the house, John-Gray."

"You go ahead. I'll come in a minute." He waited for them to be out of sight then lifting the bottle saluted his father, grandfather, Uncle Szekeres, Meeshee Kemenche, Mr. Bonyak and all the rest knowing that they too beheld the land that had been so very far off. He took another swig of the bourbon. Somehow it seemed to taste like his grandfather's plum brandy.

A Curse on Details

By 9:30 on Monday he was in their farm office, a walled-off room in the storage building where the insulation looked like a dirty eiderdown stapled to the uprights. Behind him an air conditioner set into the wall kept the office bearable even in over 100 degree temperatures. It was a noisy air conditioner but it could not drown out the choir of the Benedictine nuns of Saint Michael's Abbey singing *Mario Stabat* and *Alleluia lapis revolutus est*, the song of Mary Magdalene first crying at the tomb then with joy announcing the Resurrection. He needed to hear her joy at a time when the secular culture of death, like some poison, had seeped into the Church's lifeblood, affecting her orthodoxy and with it her centuries-old liturgy, forgetting that there is only one Liturgy and the Holy Spirit is its life.

The Church's music had changed too. One seldom heard Plainsong, Bach, Spirituals, the Requiems of Mozart, Beethoven and Faure; Buxtehude's organ music for the liturgical seasons of Easter and Pentecost, or Sabine Baring-Gould's rousing hymns. Ignoring the riches of centuries, church music had been reduced for the most part to indoor campfire songs as if the churches in the United States were striving to become Crystal Palaces or to pattern themselves on TV's show-business services with their gospel of material success. At the beginning of the 21st century it wasn't the Visigoths, Mongols or Turks who were taking over the Western churches to use as stables for their horses, but the results were the same. This secular takeover was not happening in Africa and Asia Where Christians did not meet to discuss the rightness of the inclusive language or the efficacy of homosexuality in the laity and clergy. Neither did they discuss the appropriateness of abortions or the passing to the State the responsibility for the hungry and the weak. They based their lives on the scriptures and were murdered for confessing Christ as Lord.

The nuns had stopped singing. He got up to put on another CD. Faure's *Ave verum corpus* engulfed him. It hailed the *true body of Christ, born of the Virgin Mary, verily suffered, sacrificed upon the Cross for mankind.* The music lifted him up to float freely in the presence of God where vanities and arrogance vanished and where the only reality was love that filled him with awe. He wanted to build a church where God the Father, God the Son, God the Holy Spirit could be preached without fear of contradiction. Yesterday on the way to Mass at the Shriner's Club, rented for their Sunday services, his wife told him to stop torturing himself with impossibilities.

"Be thankful All Saints can afford to rent a place for us to meet in," Meg said. "We are too few to be thinking of building. The Shriner's Club is a step up from meeting in each other's homes."

"Not much of a step." We can no longer say that we are in the world but not of it, he thought.

"I know how much you miss Saint Michael's." She patted his hand.

He remembered how hard it was to leave St. Michael's, their old parish, to give up the sanctuary with its smells of candles, prayer books, hymnals, the wood of the pews, kneelers, and slate floors. But even worse was leaving behind the love he had encountered in the Eucharist that united them. The smell of fresh brewed coffee could still conjure up nostalgia for the lost fellowship.

Ten years ago he had gone back to St. Michael's to ask for their 1928 Books of Common Prayer and their 1940 Hymnals. It was hard to be a stranger in a place where his wife and daughter had looked after the altar for twenty years and he and his son had mowed the lawns once a week in the growing season. He had been on the Vestry the year they stood in front of the delegates to the Florida Diocesan Conference and sang the Doxology in thanksgiving for Saint Michael's becoming a self-sustaining parish.

He knew where the storage room was. He had spent hours there with his brethren preparing for their yard sales. He wasn't asking for charity from strangers. "Sorry but you can't have them," the woman said. They had once been on an outreach committee together. "Why can't we'? They are no use to Saint Michael's anymore." He couldn't remember her name. She used to sit with her husband in the pew in front of them. "They have been earmarked for recycling," a youngish man said. "It was the vestry's decision." "But why recycle them? At All Saints we still use them." The hymnals and prayer books had been dumped on the floor like a sack of coal.

"I know who you are," the man said. It sounded like an accusation. "We still have the old photos of the 'Founding Fathers.'" "We miss your family," the woman said. "Thank you

Susan." He had remembered her name. "And how is Charlie?" "1 don't know. We divorced soon after y'all left."

Among the prayer books and hymnals were some of the kneelers he had built when the fellowship hall was their sanctuary with folding chairs and homemade kneelers. He picked up one, daring them to stop him.

On top of the computer desk in his office were photos of Meg, their children and grandchildren. In one photo Anne, his daughter-in-law, was riding Zoltan, their great Hanoverian dressage champion. Zoltan was named after a distant Hungarian cousin. Meg always said their lifestyle was a blessing that allowed them to create living memorials in the naming of their horses. His wife collected blessings the way some people collected antiques. A blessing could be a friend's offer to taste a bowl of salmon soup garnished with dill from his garden or God's peace that passeth all understanding. When in his fifties they still had a pack of hounds, he was always the first to hear their rabies tags jingle as they emerged from the woods. His children used to say that he couldn't possibly hear them, that it was only his mind tuned in to the hounds' brain-waves. His hearing had always been acute. Another blessing, Meg would say.

Pulling aside the curtains he looked outside. The sky was overcast, promising rain as it had done for the last three weeks without results. They had to put off fertilizing the pastures. It was difficult to see any blessing in that.

He opened the door and stepped into the aisle flanked by the stalls. From the tack-room he took a cupful of cat food and poured it onto the cement floor. Casper gave a short greeting on his way down from the hayloft. Milly emerged from one of the empty stalls.

Turning on the overhead fans he sat down on a canvas chair, the type film directors used on movie sets. The chair had been given to him by Charlotte, his friend of over thirty years. She thought he was too old to perch on feed bins while waiting for the horses to finish eating. Now sitting with his legs outstretched listening to the clicking of the overhead fans he wished that his eidetic memory complete with built-in videos, had been dulled by old age so that he wouldn't have to replay every inflection in Charlotte's voice that had transformed him yesterday from a man wanting to build for the glory of God into a boy of five promising to be good if only Santa would bring him a church.

"Actually," she had said, "beyond wishful thinking do you have any assets? Any money? Any ideas about fund raising? Bank loans? Those little details are really necessary. "

He couldn't bring himself to say that he was praying, because to his shame prayer would have sounded inconsequential even to his own ears in the vicinity of fund raising and bank loans. Charlotte, whose first husband had been a banker, had looked at him with love and pity. He knew—it wasn't for the first time— that she was thinking it was too bad he hadn't been born with a bit of Lancashire common sense. To paraphrase an old cigarette ad: *You can take Charlotte out of Lancashire but you can't take Lancashire out of Charlotte.*

He had woken up in the middle of the night knowing that he should have shot down Charlotte's "Lancashire common sense" with the howitzer of a Voltaire quotation. Earlier this morning sitting on Meg's side of the bed next to the telephone, he pushed number 3 on the automatic dialer.

"Good morning, good morning," Charlotte was singing into the receiver.

"It's me, Charlotte. It's too early to sing. Meg is just now grinding the coffee beans.

"Do you mean you get fresh-ground coffee every morning. You're spoiled."

"Do you have a minute?" "Of course. Our coffee beans are already ground. By Publix."

"I just want to zap you with a bit of Voltaire. Listen carefully: *'A curse on details; they are vermin which kill great works'*. What does your Lancashire common sense have to say about that?"

"I don't like Voltaire. I don't like his philosophy. He brushed aside anything that didn't fit his theories."

"Where do you get that ?"

"Edward Gibbon."

"Who?"

"Edward Gibbon. *The Decline and Fall of the Roman Empire* as all schoolboys should know. I have to go. You're giving me a headache. I can't be intellectual before my first cup of coffee."

From where he was sitting under one of the overhead fans the feeding horses standing across the aisle with their heads bent into their buckets looked like the backs of empty pews ranked in front of an altar. Beyond them seven deer grazed at the edge of the woods. The deer were of all sizes, the largest one holding its tail straight up like a cricket bat. His grandchildren's three ponies, Frodo, Fancy and Rosie stood among them like unicorns in a painting of Eden they had seen in a 'Stately Home' in England. Charlotte was right. He was but a child pretending to be an old man without wit enough to build a sand-castle not to speak of a church, the uncalled-for gift he wanted to give to enable him to bear the unmerited Mercy and Goodness that had stood by him all the days of his life. In the woods coyotes began to vocalize sounding like coonhounds treeing their quarry. The deer froze in their various poses as if playing Statues. The Old Testament lesson for this morning had been the passage where Gideon asks for a sign.

And Gideon said to God, Let not Thine anger be hot against me, and I will speak but this once: let me prove, I pray thee, but this once with the fleece.

This was the second time that Gideon had asked for a sign with the fleece yet Gideon's faith was the same conviction that made the walls of Jericho tumble down, that allowed Rahab the harlot and her family to live, faith that stopped the mouths of lions. Asking for signs wasn't considered strange before Dr. Freud and the subconscious mind when Psyche was still only a princess beloved by Cupid. A very different world from that of the 21st century where mother love was described by a geneticist as only a negative gene safeguarding her own genes.

He got up, switched off the overhead fan, turned off the spigot that regulated the water troughs and entered the aisle, closing the first gate behind him. The coyotes stopped singing, the deer vanished, the cats climbed up into the empty hayloft, the goldfishes in the nearest water-trough came up to the surface in expectation of their breakfast when the horses started to drink. Whistling for Sussie and her four-month-old daughter, Tilly, he opened the right-hand-side gate turning them out to their pasture. Next, Nonie—named after his son John's beloved Sunday school teacher of thirty-five years ago—stopped for her blessing, then came Nicomas who was born in the moonlight. All the *Holsteiner* fillies' names had to start with an N this year.

The ponies could be named anything the children liked. Bitsy stopped for a moment to have her forehead petted then trotted out into her pasture followed by Aileen, a part Connemara, two weeks her junior Aileen was the heroine in the *Turfcutter's Donkey*, one of their great grandmother's favorites, the book that had to be read aloud in an Irish brogue.

He closed the connecting gate to the barn, then moved the canvas chair next to the wall. The unchanging ritual performed twice a day reassured him when even the Church had become subject to epigenesis, the theory of an approximately stepwise process by which genetic information, as modified by environmental influences, is translated into the substance and behavior of an organism. The emphasis was on the outside cultural influences. He needed a sign, an assurance that he wasn't a blind man pretending vision in seeing each human action and all human history in the light of an imminent God that had made his life a gift and not a simple, statistically explainable fact.

He closed the tack-room door. Hearing it, Casper came to the edge of the hayloft to investigate. A noisy jay sounded off on the large sycamore behind him. He left, opening and closing yet another gate. Gates kept the horses out of harm's way.

He heard the mourning doves' call that had always filled him with a nameless desire which he now understood to be a longing for evidence of things not seen, the incomprehensible, inassimilable Other who also gave Himself as the God of Abraham, Flesh and Blood nailed to the cross. *Sursum corda*. He was an old man desperate for communication beyond language, words beyond prose that would become doves of sacrifice flying toward the Throne. His own words, in their imperfection, always crashed like blackened, useless rocket-boosters.

In the distance the trees around his house moved in the breeze like giants lifting their arms toward the sky.

Hear the voice of my humble petition when I hold up my hands towards the mercy-seat of thy holy temple. He raised his hands toward the sky.

On the road a passing UPS truck driver tapped his horn in greeting.

The Sound of Many Waters

For the last seven years they had spent Thanksgiving week on St. George Island, a barrier island in the Gulf of Mexico, southeast of the Apalachicola River and the town and bay named after it. This was their son's Thanksgiving gift to his family and friends—a week's stay in one of the two-story houses on the beach front. In the past friends had come from as far away as Scotland. This year John had rented a house on Sailfish Drive called *Brisa De Mar*, a large house with five bedrooms, five baths, and two living areas. Like the other houses, this too was built on stilts, and it took true grit and determination on the rainy evening of their arrival to carry their luggage and boxes of supplies up the countless stairs to the living area on the top floor. He and Meg had been dispatched on Sunday to open the house. The rest of the family would arrive on Wednesday after school let out.

197

Monday morning was clear and chilly. The glass doors leading to the top deck were shut. Sitting in the living room on one of the overstuffed love-seats reading the lessons for the day, he couldn't keep from glancing up at the Gulf, an enormous slightly tilted oblong mirror reflecting the gray sky. At the furthest rim where the sky created a continuous seam, a fine-pointed brush touched it just then with a tentative stroke of purple that began to run, bleaching into violet.

The second reading was Revelation, Chapter 1:

And in the midst of seven candlesticks one like unto the Son of man, clothed with a garment down to the foot, and girt about the paps with a golden girdle. His head and his hairs were white like wool, as white as snow; and his eyes were like flame of fire; and his feet unto fine brass as if they burned in a furnace; and his voice as the sound of many waters.

Meg came in and opened the doors leading to the deck. The sound of the endlessly rolling waves filled the room.

And I turned to see the voice that spake with me.

For forty-five years he had been conjuring up and holding on to that other morning on England's Devonshire coast where amidst the thunder of the rolling shingle he had heard a still small voice that freed him from the vacuum he had condemned himself to at the death of his father, and upheld by the deaths of his comrades, that transformed him into a sterile, unfeeling being, set apart from any vulnerable living creature. By the end of World War II, that brought on more death, rape, and torture, he was in a caveman-like state, functioning only to satisfy his basic hungers, he no longer remembered the beauty of feelings, sensations that went beyond wants.

Five years after the ending of World War II, he had escaped the communists in Hungary finding refuge in England to become one of the "floor people" working in coal-mines, gasworks, cotton mills and as institutional kitchen porters. The extraordinary, the miraculous can happen anywhere. He had met Meg, who had taken him out of his self-imposed isolation. The astonishing thing was that she was brave enough to marry him and that her parents had given their blessing.

"It's a lovely view," Meg said. "Our children are spoiling us. I hope the weather stays sunny for them."

"I don't hear any gulls."

That morning in Devonshire when his sins of commission, omission and the guilt thereof had been lifted from him, he was standing on the terrace of his in-laws' large Victorian house (that because of an unexplained whimsy was called "The Croft"), hearing the gulls shriek as they flew around the church steeple reassuring him that he wasn't hallucinating, that the reality of God's love was no more outlandish than the reality of gravity and oxygen that he had taken for granted all his life knowing without conscious thought that he couldn't live without them.

Having eaten breakfast in the huge kitchen—in October the only permanently warm place in the house—he, Meg and his in-laws had moved to the equally large but chilly dining room. His mother-in-law had switched on two of the four bars of the electric heater standing in the fireplace (two bars having been deemed adequate to banish the autumn chill), then they knelt down and began to pray.

Kneeling in the company of these people whose lives witnessed to that other reality eliminated the need to seek a scientific or psychological explanation for the still small voice, a voice that would remain with him all his tomorrows, yet kneeling in the dining room had embarrassed him. Their settlement in Hungary was staunchly Reformed and Calvinists did not kneel. His mother would not have been embarrassed to kneel since she was a French Roman Catholic. Early in their marriage, his father, wanting his bride to feel at home, had a chapel built for her and engaged a resident priest to say Mass. His parents' marriage had come about as one of the side-effects of history. After the signing of the Armistice in 1918, there had been a communist takeover of short duration in Hungary. His father, a "white" officer, had fled to the French-held part of the country, where he fell in love with the French commandant's seventeen-year-old daughter. Both families thought their marriage—not to speak of the civil ceremony—unacceptable. Acceptance came only when he was born and was baptized in the Reformed faith. His sister, the firstborn, was a Roman Catholic like their mother.

He put on a jacket and went outside to stand on the deck. A formation of stately pelicans flew by surveying the changing color of the Gulf. At the furthest horizon the sky was a rising curtain on the staging of a new day. Where purple had been bleached into violet the sky was now indigo turning into gold; Nature's vesting for the coming Advent season. Then it was all light and on top of the water a wide band of quicksilver was rushing toward him.

That other morning, kneeling close to the fireplace to absorb the meager heat of the two electric bars, he had marveled at the straight back of his ancient, sixty-five-year-old father-in-law. Now he was at least fifteen years older than his father-in-law had been then, when their world was still framed by the bells ringing for Morning Prayer, Holy Communion and Evensong. That world was as distant now as the sepia photos of his ancestors from the end of the 19th and the beginning of the 20th centuries, pictures of men, women and children dressed in awkward clothes and equally uncomfortable-looking uniforms that had since become the foundation for some of the 21st century's retro-fashion ideas.

If he needed a marker for the beginning of his changed world, it was the shock he had received in his dentist's waiting room when he picked up the April 8th, 1966 issue of T I M E with the cover asking: **Is God Dead?**

In 1966 he was a forty-three-year-old survivor of World War II, who had seen nihilism in Europe destroying traditional culture that allowed Nazism, Communism and Fascism to rush in and take over. At the age of sixteen, he, like all the other gymnasium students in the Europe of his generation, was taught that Nihilism in Nietzsche's view was the dormant presence in the foundation of European culture, culture that had reached a dead end caused by the unresolved search for meaning through philosophical skepticism and modern science's evolutionary and heliocentric theory. In Nietzsche's view Nihilism was the necessary coming destiny. In the heliocentric theory the sun represented the center. God was dead.

At school Nietzsche's ideas were counterbalanced by Kant's philosophy and by his teachers' speculations that Nietzsche's brain had been damaged by cancer, or a syphilitic infection or even that his madness was caused by psychological maladjustment brought on by his own philosophy.

In 1966, when T I M E an ordinary, slightly boring mass circulation American publication could ask the question: "Is God dead?" without eliciting a reaction from his fellow patients in the waiting room, he knew that the Word that was in the beginning was no longer heard.

The effect of the Novocain and the T I M E shock had worn off at about the same time. He remembered Mrs. Hall's class at Swarthmore (in '51 he had been given a special scholarship) where he learned about the Enlightenment and the Reverend Ralph Waldo Emerson's : "Nothing is sacred but the integrity of your mind." Not many years later Flannery O'Connor wrote: "*When Emerson said he could no longer celebrate the Lord's Supper unless the bread and wine were removed, an important step in the vaporization of religion in America had taken place.*" The *vaporization* was even more visible in the 21st century, where Emerson's ideas had become the accepted philosophy and the established religion of the majority. T.S. Eliot's: *The dripping blood our only drink, the bloody flesh our only food,* their received gift, their common bond, had to sit in the back of the bus. Worldly sophistication—if it viewed the Body of Christ at all—advertised it as not unlike some healthier bologna variety that could be sliced very thin and was easy to digest.

At about the same time the study of literature was reduced to a sublet of Freudian psychology, or all writing had to be viewed through a Marxist looking-glass followed by a sociological approach to literary criticism. Literature, the living soul of nations, was condemned to death by a philosophical movement called deconstruction.

de.con.struc.tion *(de'kan struk'shan) a philosophical and critical movement, starting in the 1960's and esp. applied to the study of literature, that questions all traditional assumptions about the ability of language to represent reality and emphasizes that a text has no stable reference or identification because words essentially only refer to other words and therefore a reader must approach a text by eliminating any metaphysical or ethnocentric assumptions through an active role of construction, etymology, puns and other word play.*

He took off his jacket and draped it on one of the plastic chairs on the deck. It had warmed up enough to be pleasant in shirtsleeves. On the boardwalk between their house and the next, a group of young people emerged, jostling each other flowing around one or two hand-holding couples who solemnly walked down toward the beach. When they reached the sand their leader, not much older than the rest, halted them. The shouting and jumping about ceased abruptly. Forming a circle not unlike a football huddle, they began to pray. His first reaction was to ridicule but he was saved from it by remembering reading Carl Jung's: "The opposite of love is not hate but lust for power with which to diminish others."

The huddle broke up. A girl threw a frisbee that, aided by the slight breeze, was spinning toward the waves when a young man out of nowhere flew almost horizontally toward it and caught the disk before it hit the ground. A frisky, black Labrador puppy was let off its leash and went racing up and down the shore attacking the wavelets. Further down the beach a little boy was leaning over a dead bird. Calling to his sister he began pulling on the entrails, then they squatted down like haruspices practicing divination. The puppy joined them. Before they had a chance to utter a prophetic word their distraught mother arrived, put a red leash on the puppy and shooed the children away. Laughing, they ran off toward their still unknown future.

Beyond the people on the beach, the horizon was dotted with fantastic, metaphysical sea creatures, their wings stretched wide, gliding toward the passage cut between the end of St. George and the next island: shrimp boats coming in with the morning catch. The last of the mist was blotted by the sun, and the white, square shape of the town of Apalachicola, backlit by the blue of the sky, rose to form the centerpiece of the bay. He was overwhelmed by the beauty of his surroundings that made him afraid the same way he was afraid in Vienna in 1946 after he had crawled through the barbed wire of the Hungarian-Austrian border, then, slipping by the Soviet checkpoints, had arrived at the Hotel Wandl, reputed to be taking in guests without passports. The hotel was located in the First District, the International zone, close to St. Stephan's cathedral. He got into his freezing room—there was no heat in the hotel unless you had your own stove—and lying down on the lumpy bed covered himself with all the blankets he could find. In one of the neighboring rooms somebody was playing a cello. He didn't recognize the somber music but its haunting beauty nullified the last thirty hours that had taken away his remaining shred of humanity to turn him into a terrified hare fleeing from the beaters toward the waiting guns. He was well aware that his chances were even of being taken back across the border to be shot or to end up further East in the GULAG, yet at that moment what he had feared most was that the music would stop and he would never hear it again.

"Breakfast will be ready in five minutes," Meg called.

He went to the edge of the deck to have a last look before going in. There were more people on the beach now walking toward or coming back from the west end of the Island. The Labrador puppy, free again, was attacking the wavelets followed by the little boy and his sister; their mother, picking up shells, lagged far behind. He recognized some members of the Christian youth group among the strollers and the marching health walkers in the usual gallimaufry of colors, sizes and ages of people on Florida's beaches. Looking down on them he was thinking of all the miracles that had made it possible for him to be one in the mix here to celebrate Thanksgiving.

Meg came outside and stood next to him.

"Let's eat breakfast on the deck," she said. "We have such a lovely view."

The Long Journey Home

For their 60th anniversary their son presented them with plane tickets to England. They would go next month, September, the perfect time to escape Florida's continuing heat. Their first night, Saturday night, would be spent in Sudbury, Derbyshire, at a Bread & Breakfast, since all their village friends who had participated in their July wedding sixty years ago had moved on to All Saints churchyard. His wife's father, one of the former rectors of All Saints, was also buried there. He had dug the grave for his father-in-law's ashes by the side door where he used stand talking with his parishioners after the services. The grave had been marked only with a rosebush to be cared for by the village to comply with his widow's, the beloved "crazy American lady's" wishes.

On Sunday they hoped to attend the ten-thirty Harvest Festival at All Saints then repair with some of the parishioners to

The Vernon Arms for a pub lunch before driving on to Northumberland to stay at Holmhead Farm Guest House in the vicinity of Hadrian's Wall. It belonged to the daughter of their closest Sudbury friends now resting in the churchyard. The eighty-mile-long Wall, an impressive civil engineering work undertaken by the Romans during their occupation of Britain, A.D 85-211, was a witness to the achievement of a great civilization, the visible remains of the furthest frontier of the Roman Empire.

Sixty years ago when he first laid eyes on Sudbury the day before their wedding, he was in a heightened state that made his Hungarian accent sound like a happy pagan hailing Dionysus with a dithyramb. For centuries this lovely English village was a Vernon family estate-village that prevented it from becoming either rundown or twee. Anthony Trollope, the 19th century English novelist, couldn't have foreseen, when in his capacity as a postal inspector in Ireland he had introduced Britain to the landmark red pillar-boxes, that a 20th century Lord Vernon would so thoroughly despise that he had ordered the only telephone booth in the village to be hidden in an out-of the-way location. The British Post Office red clashed with the Hall's and The Vernon Arms' mellow brick construction.

The Bishop of Derby had officiated at their wedding along with Meg's Uncle Ronald, a High Church priest with a beautifully lazy voice, and his own father-in-law with his deep Cambridge intonation. The communist government of Hungary following the Soviet Union's tirade of petty revenge, decided to punish the escapee son by denying an exit visa for his mother a French Roman Catholic, who would have approved of the ornate vestments worn by the Bishop and Uncle Ronald.

He had been unable to eat at the wedding breakfast served in the garden. Later he was on the verge of crying when somebody told him that his wife had already changed into traveling clothes. It was the first time anybody had called Meg his wife. Then Lord Vernon's chauffeur, Mr. Roberts, came with the Rolls to take them to the small train station by the river Dove on the road to Tutbury.

For Meg, Sudbury had been home for only a short time. When her father had become All Saints' rector she was living mostly in London as a university student. Sudbury had meant reassuring family weekends, the reassurance coming mostly from her father who implicitly trusted her judgment. Later on this trust played a part in her family's acceptance of the "enemy alien" kitchen porter as her future husband.

* * * * * *

His own reaction to their coming journey was colored by a hefty book entitled : *SAINTS, A YEAR IN FAITH AND ART*. In the mornings while eating breakfast at the kitchen counter it had given them a new look at church history told through the lives of her saints, gloriously illustrated by the likes of Durer, Filipino Lippi, Botticelli, El Greco, Titian, Murillo. The saint designated for a particular day had usually died a martyr's death, killed in some gruesome, horrific way.

August 2nd was dedicated to pope Stephen I.
Saint Stephen I succeeded Lucius I as pope during the reign of Emperor Valerian. During his three-year pontificate (254-57) he faced the problem of the readmission of the 'lapsi', lapsed Christians who had renounced their faith out of fear and now asked to return to the Church. He too had been a *lapsi*. The memory of it had become an unwanted 'Spam' he was unable to clear. It had dredged up the long-buried cowardice of the man who as a boy *knew* that he too, along with the other martyrs, would have defied Nero and the

207

panem et circenses-shouting proletariat. At sixteen he had memorized Rimbaud's *Les Illuminations: "I am the saint at prayer on the terrace like the peaceful beasts that graze down to the sea of Palestine."* It didn't matter that he wasn't aspiring to become a military hero. There was nobody he could talk to about his longing to become a saint. It was taken for granted that at eighteen he would enter the military academy like his father and all of the men of his family.

After that Saint Stephen's day reading, he came to feel that a transcendent bookkeeper had appeared to tote up his sins and for punishment reproduce them in primary colors. He knew full well that the statistical shortness of his remaining years would not allow him time enough to soften the images with a lot of mixing and fudging or simply to cover his worst sins with a psychiatric pentimento to stop the old *lapsi*-self from waking him at night to ask if he would ever again deny God to avoid physical pain.

* * * * * *

World War II ended for him and the survivors of the 2nd Hungarian Armored Division on their long retreat from the Dnieper region on April Fools' Day, 1945, in the town of Sopron close to the Austrian border. Their medical staff took over a large girls' boarding school run by a teaching order of nuns. The doctors hung a Red Cross flag, set up treatment and hospital rooms, and prayed that the Germans would not push back and the Red Army would not come in to slaughter them or ship them off to one of their labor camps.

At 13 hrs. they heard several Russian T-34 tanks pull up in front of their hospital. The Russians were shouting to each other then they started to bring in their wounded.

He left the hospital a few days after the Russians arrived to search for his mother. In six days he had made it to Budapest by alternately jumping on freight trains and hiding. After a week of searching, feeling as if he were trying to glue together some old broken crockery that nobody had any interest in he had found his mother living in an air raid shelter on the Pest side. She told him that his sister was staying in the ruins of their villa in Buda.

In August he found a job knocking down damaged plaster cherubs and roses from the high ceiling of a coffeehouse on the Pest side facing the ruins of Chain bridge that the Germans had blown up before departing. He was also the watchman which temporarily allowed him to use the coffeehouse's address. The owner, a survivor of Auschwitz with a sense of humor, when finding out that besides soldiering he was a poet, called the bowls of beef broth with stale bread and the burned coffee that couldn't be sold to the customers (black market toffs and their women) his honorarium.

On Monday of his second week the owner hired another worker to speed up the process so that the plasterers could start. The new worker, Peter (surnames could be liabilities) was a slight, blond man in his late thirties, friendly and at the same time distant. When he had asked about his military service it turned out that they both knew the Roman Catholic chaplain of the destroyed 1st Hungarian Armored division. Two days later he still didn't know much about Peter other than that he was a good worker who didn't mind swinging his hammer at the damaged plaster cherubs, roses, satyrs and fleeing nymphs.

Friday morning the sun was shining and he was told to take down the plywood shutters to let in the light—there was no glass to be had as yet to replace the windows. Peter was already up on a plank that rested on two tall stepladders wielding his hammer, his dark trousers streaked with plaster dust. He himself was halfway up the ladder when the sun's rays converged on Peter as if he were an invading bomber caught by antiaircraft spotlights. He resembled a saint in an altar painting he had seen in Florence on a school holiday before the war.

"*Ladatur Jesu Christi*," he said, meaning it as a jest.

"*In aeternum, amen*," Peter said, his right hand making the sign of the cross.

Two weeks later Peter told him about a "floating" church that met for Mass in some of the parks on the Buda side.

On Sunday he walked fifteen kilometers from the coffeehouse crossing a pontoon bridge to Buda. Walking down Filler Street where his artist cousin Zoltan used to have his *atelier*, he skirted paving-stone redoubts where empty machine-gun belts coiled snake-like round boots and parts of uniforms black with blood. Most of the bodies had been removed though some body parts must have remained hidden under the torn blankets nobody wanted: he could smell the rotting flesh that mingled with the smell of charred wood. He crossed the wide avenue that led toward Huvosvolgy with its chestnut trees and elegant villas where once upon a time successful Hungarians had lived until their homes were requisitioned by the Gestapo and their Hungarian Arrow Cross Party allies. Now, and for the foreseeable future, the villas were to be occupied by high-ranking Red Army and NKVD officers. He clambered up the embankment and across the tramlines with its twisted rails then slid down the other side and entered a jungle of overgrown bushes and shattered trees that had been a well-tended park before the bombs started raining down and Budapest had become a battlefield. Some of the denuded trees pointed black accusing fingers at the cloudless sky. The Buda side had been the last German holdout. Hitler's promised relief never arrived. When the last of the surviving Germans tried to retreat toward the west, they were slaughtered.

He had reached an unexpected clearing shaped like the Roman coliseum in their Latin textbook that at the age of twelve, had made him fantasize about martyrdom coinciding with their mother's announcement that her children would not be put into chronological straitjackets, where their ages dictated what they may read or listen to. The listening part had come first: Wagner's *Ring Cycle*, which she performed in the music room, reciting the libretto while accompanying herself on the grand Boesendorfer piano. She sang all the roles, stopping occasionally to point out that a particular part should be sung several octaves lower or higher. The music and the stories made him think that true love must cause unbearable pain.

The clearing had a bench with a sawed-off back, snug against a wall of bushes. The only sounds came from an unseen military convoy up on the road. He was sniffing the air like an animal.

The Russian soldiers smoked *mahorka*, the chopped-up stems of tobacco leaves rolled in whatever paper was handy. He could smell them a long way off.

The military convoy had passed. There was no way to classify the silence that followed. Then he heard a soft, stealthy movement and Peter appeared. Without acknowledging him, Peter put on his stole and briskly transformed the bench into an altar. Men, women and children materialized from the jungle. No greetings were exchanged, nobody spoke.

In nomine Patris et Filie, et Spiritus Sancti. Amen. The priest crossed himself. *Introibo ad altere Dei.*

Ad Deum, qui laetificat juventum meam, the server said, standing at the right side of the altar.

Judica me, Deus,...

Judge me, O God, the priest prayed, *and distinguish my cause from the nation that is not holy ...*

211

My nation, he thought, took Christ's Cross sharpening it into an 'Arrow Cross' to join the Swastika in sanctioning the deportation and murder of Hungarian Jews, Gypsies, and all those who opposed them until hate grew to destroy Budapest, the once beautiful city, cutting it in half by blowing up the bridges. The new occupiers fit perfectly the altered landscape with their sanctioned rape and random roundup of men to be shipped off to one of their labor camps. Just as the Swastika and the Arrow Cross had done, the Hammer & Sickle had collected eager local support to join some of the most vicious civilian communists, the former leaders of the first communist regime in 1919 that had lasted only five months.

Kyrie eleison.

Kyrie eleison.

Kyrie eleison.

Christe eleison.

Christe eleison.

Christe eleison.

Indulgentiam, absolutionem, et remisissionem, the priest intoned with his hand uplifted, peccatorum nostrorum tribuatnobis omnipotens, et miserricors Dominus.

Amen.

Kneeling in the dirt among the newly sprouted weeds he was doubly illegal in this clearing (he was a Calvinist like his father), waiting to receive the Eucharist that the Church had refused him with the contrivance of his own Roman Catholic mother.

Dominus vobiscum.

Et cum spiritu tuo. The priest, turning, made the sign of the cross over them.

Indulgentiam, absolutionem, et remissionem peccatorum nostrum tribuatnobis omnipotens, et misericors Dominus.

Amen.

Dominus vobiscum.
Et cum spiritu tuo.

After receiving the Eucharist at the makeshift altar his body moved in an involuntary spiral as if trying to overcome earth's gravity and the equally powerful pull of the culture of death he had lived in these past two years. For the first time in his life he had experienced Church as the Body of Christ. His own fears, agonies and depredations that the war and his own fallen nature had brought on receded in this moment of sanctification.

Ite, missa est.
Deo gratias.

Thanking God was a huge sigh, then with the susurration of the wings of great birds the congregation flew away. Feeling the closeness of his father, who had died at the age of forty-six at the beginning of the war, it seemed as if the Budapest opera house's great fire-curtain, that always descended after the final act, had been lifted.

* * * * * *

Their son's anniversary present reminded him of his own mortality: *This will be the last time I'll see Sudbury*. He wondered if walking in the churchyard reading the names of their friends he would be able to conjure up their faces and their strong North Country voices, their regional peculiarities that had made them seem so utterly different from who he was sixty years ago. Their acceptance of him, an EVW (European Voluntary Worker) was a new experience, something that he hadn't encountered as a four-loom weaver in a cotton mill in Lancashire or as a laborer in Saint Albans's gasworks nor as a kitchen porter in Shenley mental hospital.

213

On Sunday the parking lot was full. Cars were parked on both sides of the main Sudbury road. People passed in front of Sudbury Hall moving toward the immense lawn between it and the lake to celebrate 'Derbyshire Day', a gimmick invented by one of the radio stations to drum up business for the National Trust. Merchants had set up their tables on the lawn and there was even an organ grinder with a fake monkey. The Vernon Arms, the only pub in the village, was filled up with 'visitors'.

The church bells were ringing when he and Meg crossed the road from the parking lot walking straight on toward All Saints on their way to the 10:30 Harvest Festival service. They were the only people heading for the church.

As always, on entering All Saints after a long hiatus, he checked the tablet fastened on the back wall of the church with the names of the former rectors, his father-in-law among them going back to the Georgian period. The sanctuary was empty but he could hear voices coming from the choir room. All Saints, a large church, was decorated for the Harvest Festival: the pulpit, lectern, font, organ loft and all the deep window ledges were bedecked with dahlias, asters, Michaelmas daisies, roses, all the late summer flowers as well as wheat, fruit and vegetables. There was a plaited loaf of bread on the altar.

By the time the bells stopped ringing, the congregation had assembled—nine people—outnumbered by the twelve-member choir. Instead of the rector, who was also in charge of six other parishes, a lay minister read Morning Prayer.

The singing was lovely.

* * * * * *

His grandson, in his second year at the University of Florida, was reading Shakespeare's *The Tempest*. In an epilogue, Prospero, the right Duke of Milan, recites: . . . *Let me not/ Since I have my dukedom got,/And pardoned the deceiver, dwell/In this bare Island by your spell* . . . Since returning from England even the mention of a "bare Island" could produce memories of Northumberland with its rock walls surrounding vivid green pastures. In the mornings from the upstairs window of their stone house in the village of Greenhead with the ruins of the fourteenth century Thirwall Castle in the background, they had watched the large grayish-white oval of the sleeping sheep. Then, at the signal of the rising sun, the sheep separated into small grazing groups slowly spreading over the pasture. Soon a shepherd appeared on a small four-wheel utility vehicle with his dog sitting behind him. When the vehicle stopped, the dog hopped down, moved the sheep onto the next pasture, came back, hopped up again and they were off, driving out of sight.

Often they saw groups of walkers pass by, some of them intent on walking the whole eighty miles of Hadrian's Wall. Just a few miles from Greenhead, at Housesteads, a Roman fort with a clear view of both the North and the South, still clung to the hillside. Down below a museum was filled with the reliquary of the Roman past among which were the discarded leather shoes and sandals of the legionnaires miraculously preserved in a bog. There were also models of some of the sections of the Wall and its strongholds with the legionnaires' housing. Watching the half-hour video presentation he flew with an eagle following the Wall toward Vindolanda, overwhelmed by the magnificence and glory of Hadrian's Empire. Once again he had found in antiquity a man he could admire. Hadrian was a foremost patron of artists and architects, had rebuilt the Parthenon, knew classical Greek, was an accomplished poet, composer and musician.

On their fourth day back in Florida, reading up on Roman history of the period, the image of the cultivated, intellectual emperor had drastically changed to reveal Hadrian the tyrant who, while vowing to rebuild Jerusalem as a gift to the Jews, had built an edifice to Jupiter on Temple Mount and had forbidden the practice of Judaism. The ensuing uprising led by Shimon Bar-Kokba had taken Hadrian's legions three years to put down. The revolt had caused the Roman legions' retreat from Britannia, ending their 326-year occupation.

After crushing the rebellion, Hadrian renamed Jerusalem *Colonia Aelia Capitolonia* and the country: Syria Palestina. For punishment, all the Jews and Jewish-Christians were sold into slavery, or transported to Egypt. On pain of death they were forbidden to return. New residents from all over the empire were imported and the country had become *Juden frei*, a term used centuries later in another part of the world.

* * * * * *

Waking up Monday morning six weeks after their anniversary visit to England, he got his calculator to tell him how much time had elapsed since working with Peter the R.C. priest on the ceiling of the coffeehouse on the Pest side of Chain Bridge. He had never learned his surname or found out if he had survived those early horrific years of communist rule. He only knew that Peter had made it possible for him to experience the Church as the Body of Christ. The calculator told him it had been sixty-four years ago.

Early on in his childhood he had experienced God's love and also His disappearance. Neither his loving parents nor the presents heaped on him could fill the terrible emptiness he felt lying on his sickbed not knowing why he was abandoned. When he was up again and was taken to the park he heard Fraulein Mitzi describe him to the other nannies as a strange boy. He

216

knew she was referring to his long illness that first confined him to the nursery and later separated him from his school-age peers. Four days a week his Fraulein Mitzi took him to his tutor's apartment. It was only in fourth grade that he could go to school with other boys. His sister, following their mother who was a Roman Catholic, was taught by an order of nuns in a boarding school. When she was at home their mother used to take them both to her Inner City church on the Pest side of the city. She said he needed to "hear and see the beauty of the Mass," but he had to stay behind when they went up to the altar to receive the Eucharist, left behind like a newly purchased horse quarantined to keep from infecting others.

His own children and grandchildren were Americans without all the Grand Guignol he had carried like an overloaded packhorse that at times would transform a 91 milligram 'baby' aspirin rolling off the bathroom counter into a fugitive desperately trying to escape. He had lived in the United States since 1950, most of that time in Florida, becoming a citizen in 1954. He was still amazed to find that most of the native born didn't realize that the country of their birth was the only place on earth where one could 'become': no one could become French, Hungarian, Italian, Russian, German, Swedish or any of the other nationalities, but in the U.S. after the naturalization ceremony they could, in their various accents say "I am an American." They belonged, and so did he even though they lived among the strife and divisions that touched them all.

It was comforting for him to know surrounded by loving and beloved people that he was coming to the end of a long journey on his way to his true home where the sun shall not burn him by day neither the moon by night, where he would be changed in a moment, in the twinkling of an eye to be the man he was always intended to be.

Made in the USA
Lexington, KY
03 May 2014